# NANCY DREW® 147

## THE CASE OF
## THE CAPTURED QUEEN

### CAROLYN KEENE

D0110283

A MINSTREL® BOOK

Published by POCKET BOOKS
New York   London   Toronto   Sydney   Tokyo   Singapore

The sale of this book without its cover is unauthorized. If you purchased this book without a cover, you should be aware that it was reported to the publisher as "unsold and destroyed." Neither the author nor the publisher has received payment for the sale of this "stripped book."

This book is a work of fiction. Names, characters, places and incidents are products of the author's imagination or are used fictitiously. Any resemblance to actual events or locales or persons living or dead is entirely coincidental.

A MINSTREL PAPERBACK *Original*

A Minstrel Book published by
POCKET BOOKS, a division of Simon & Schuster Inc.
1230 Avenue of the Americas, New York, NY 10020

Copyright © 1999 by Simon & Schuster Inc.
Produced by Mega-Books, Inc.

All rights reserved, including the right to reproduce this book or portions thereof in any form whatsoever. For information address Pocket Books, 1230 Avenue of the Americas, New York, NY 10020

ISBN: 0-671-02175-3

First Minstrel Books printing January 1999

10  9  8  7  6  5  4  3  2  1

NANCY DREW, NANCY DREW MYSTERY STORIES, A MINSTREL BOOK and colophon are registered trademarks of Simon & Schuster Inc.

Front cover illustration by Bill Schmidt

Printed in the U.S.A.

# Contents

# THE CASE OF
# THE CAPTURED QUEEN

# 1

## The Ghost Rider

"I hope we're not late," Nancy Drew said as she eased her foot off the brake of her blue Mustang and inched the car forward a few feet. "The bus gets in at nine-thirty."

Nancy's friend George Fayne glanced at her watch. "We've got plenty of time, Nan," she said. "Thirty seconds, to be exact."

Nancy smiled. "Thirty whole seconds. What a relief." She steered the car into the right-hand lane.

The smell of exhaust filled the Mustang, and the morning sun glared brightly off the rear window of the car in front of them.

"This chess tournament has turned downtown

into one giant traffic jam," George said. "It's a much bigger deal than I thought."

"If River Heights were hosting a major volleyball tournament instead of the International Junior Masters Chess Championship, you wouldn't be so surprised," Nancy replied with a sly smile.

"Right, and if this were volleyball, I'd be playing, not watching," George said.

"That's true." Nancy held her right hand up to block the glare. She could tell it was going to be an unseasonably warm day for spring. She was glad she'd dressed in cotton shorts and a light denim jacket.

"We've got to get out of here," George said, tilting her sunglasses up on her forehead and scanning the situation. "There," she said, pointing to an alley next to the convention center. "Cut through to Riverside Park."

Nancy deftly wheeled the car into the narrow space and accelerated, missing an obstacle course of metal trash cans.

"Good driving," George said as the car popped back out into the bright sun.

"Good scouting," Nancy said as she turned down the quiet boulevard running between the park and the wide Muskoka River. She looked out the driver's-side window, then slowed the car. "Ever see anything like that before?"

"What're they doing?" George asked. "Spraying for bugs?"

Workers with shiny steel tanks strapped to their backs were spray-painting rows of alternating black and white squares on the ground in the middle of the park. Each square was about four feet on a side, and each row had eight squares.

"No, not bugs," Nancy said, laughing. "It's a chessboard. They're painting a big chessboard on the grass."

George pointed to some painted figures that stood in the shade under a couple of tall oak trees. "Those must be the game pieces. Look at how tall they are. They're bigger than real people."

Two men were unpacking a crate while a third removed a large wooden box from a truck in the parking lot. As the girls drove past, they saw the workers lift a statue of a robed woman from the crate and set it on the grass.

Nancy recognized the chess piece the figure represented immediately. It was the queen. She wore a crown and was much taller than the other pieces. She appeared to be nearly seven feet tall.

"She's so calm and beautiful," Nancy said. "I could imagine her leading a battle to protect her empire."

"Me, too," George said. "But some of the other ones look kind of creepy. I see pawns, a couple of bishops, the knights. What are the names of the pieces that look like castles? I always forget."

"Those are the rooks," Nancy said.

"Oh, right," George said. She settled back in

3

her seat. "That was amazing. This tournament's going to be fun."

Nancy pulled into the bus station parking lot behind a television news van. A crowd had gathered at the front door of the station lobby.

"Looks like we're right on time," Nancy said as she parked the car.

The two friends stepped out of the Mustang just as a silver bus with a bright red stripe down the side pulled up in front of the station. It said Chicago–River Heights above the windshield.

The crowd surged forward from the station platform, lining up beside the bus door. Young children with their parents, teenagers, and even some older people pushed against one another, holding tournament programs and ballpoint pens in the air. The bus driver forced the door open, pushing a few eager kids back. "Give us room, folks," he said.

Nancy and George stood up on the platform, out of the way. As the passengers started to get out, someone bumped into Nancy, elbowing her in the ribs. "Watch it!" a voice snapped.

Nancy turned to see Brenda Carlton, the reporter for *Today's Times*, making her way to the front of the crowd.

"I've got a story to cover, Drew," Brenda said. She tossed her head, flipping her long, dark hair back at Nancy. "What are you doing here? Are you a chess groupie?"

4

Before Nancy could answer, passengers began to step off the bus. Most of them were regular travelers from Chicago, but a few were obviously tournament participants. A little girl with red curly hair, no more than seven years old, climbed down the steps, holding her mother's hand. She had a fluffy teddy bear cradled in one arm. Camera flashes went off. Cries went up from several people in the crowd, asking for autographs.

"That must be Emily Drexler," Nancy said. "I think she's the youngest kid in the tournament."

The little girl smiled and handed the bear to her mother so she could sign her name on the back of a boy's chessboard.

More calls went up from the crowd as a tall, willowy girl stepped from the bus, carrying an overnight bag. She was followed by another girl and a plump, balding man.

"There they are," Nancy said to George. "That's Donna Winston and her sister, Danitra. Come on."

Nancy had never met Donna and Danitra, but her father, Carson Drew, a well-known criminal lawyer, had tried several big cases with their father, Howard Winston, in Chicago.

Mr. Winston had called a couple of weeks earlier to say that the whole family was coming to River Heights to watch Donna compete in the tournament. However, at the last minute Mr. and Mrs. Winston had had emergencies at their jobs and

5

couldn't make it. At Nancy's urging, Mr. Drew offered to let Donna and Danitra stay with them.

Nancy had been looking forward to meeting the Winstons, and sixteen-year-old Donna looked just as her father had said she would: slender, about five foot nine, with black shoulder-length hair cut to frame her pretty face, and chestnut-colored skin. She wore a navy blue suit that gave her the appearance of being a young businesswoman.

At fourteen, Danitra was shorter and dressed more casually than her sister. She had on a red sweatshirt and wore her hair in rows of braids, each ending with four or five red or white beads.

Nancy and George tried to get through to Donna, but the crowd was going wild. People were yelling her name, grabbing at her arms, and holding up objects for her to sign. Nancy could only wave from the platform, hoping Donna would catch sight of her and realize who she was.

Finally Nancy caught Donna's eye. "Over here!" she called.

Donna gave back a girl's pen and then held her hand out toward Nancy, pretending she was drowning in a sea of people.

Nancy reached forward and pulled Donna up onto the platform.

Donna smiled. "You must be Nancy. Thanks for rescuing me."

"It's great to finally meet you, Donna," Nancy

said. "I'm so glad you guys are going to stay with us."

"So am I," Donna said. "This is my sister," she said, gesturing toward Danitra. "And this is my high school coach, Norris Stricker."

The man's face was flushed from the heat. He wiped his face with a handkerchief and nodded to Nancy and George.

"Will you be staying with us, too?" Nancy asked Coach Stricker.

"No, no. I'm registered at the Ambassador Hotel downtown," Stricker said. "By the way, I certainly hope there's a quiet place at your house where Donna can practice."

He's certainly all business, Nancy thought. "Yes, I think so," she replied. "Donna can use my dad's office whenever she wants."

Danitra piped up. "Don't mind Coach Stricker. He thinks chess is Donna's entire life."

Stricker frowned. "I'll have none of that smart talk this week, young lady. Donna must focus on winning this tournament."

"That's right, Danitra," Donna said gently to her little sister. "Dad said you could come and watch, but I've got to focus on my matches."

At that moment Brenda Carlton pushed past Nancy again and stuck a tape recorder in Donna's face.

"Donna Winston," she said. "How does it feel

to be the number-one-ranked junior player in the United States?"

Donna shrugged. "It feels great, I guess. I play chess because I love it, so I really don't feel that much extra pressure."

Nancy saw Norris cringe.

"What about the Dutch champion, Greta van Leeuwen?" Brenda asked. "If you beat her, you could be the highest-ranked teenager in the world. How do you feel about that?"

"I'd love to be number one," Donna replied. "But I've got to win first."

"She'll win," Norris said into the microphone. "She's the best."

"That's quite a guarantee," Brenda said. She seemed to have more questions, but Donna ended the interview.

"We need to get our bags off the bus now," Donna said.

"Yes, let's get back to my house and get you settled in," Nancy suggested.

Once the crowd had finally cleared away, the girls were able to grab the Winstons' bags and load them into the Mustang.

Coach Stricker insisted on taking a cab to the hotel. "Call when you get settled in," he said to Donna. "We'll set up a practice schedule for this week."

Donna got into the front passenger seat and nodded. Nancy pulled out into the street.

"Sounds like your coach pushes you pretty hard," George said from the back.

Donna sighed as she smoothed her hair back. "He just wants to help me play better."

"He wants her to play chess twenty-four hours a day," Danitra said to Nancy and George. "He even makes her play tapes of famous chess games while she sleeps."

Nancy laughed. "Does it work?" She headed toward the park so she could show Donna the huge chess set before heading home.

Donna shook her head. "I don't know."

"How long have you been playing?" George asked.

"Since I was a little girl." Donna reached into her bag and withdrew a leather case the size of a notebook computer. "My grandfather gave this to me when I was three."

Nancy drove to the side of the park farthest from the river this time. She wanted a good look at the giant chess pieces under the trees. Up ahead, she watched a worker open a crate in the back of the truck and position a dolly to bring a chess piece down the ramp to the street.

Nancy took her eyes off the road for a split second to look over at Donna.

"Watch out!" Danitra cried from the backseat.

Nancy looked out the window in time to see what looked like a horse—a gleaming white stallion—charging right at her side of the car!

# 2

# *Unfair Warning*

Nancy stomped on the gas pedal, expecting to hear the sound of crunching metal and feel the impact of the horse.

The collision didn't come. Nancy glanced in the rearview mirror in time to see the figure of a rider on horseback pass behind the car.

"What just happened?" Donna asked. The leather case she'd been holding had fallen to the floor.

Nancy stopped the car. "I don't know, but let's find out."

George's laugh interrupted her. "Don't worry, Nancy. It was one of the big chess pieces."

The girls piled out of the car. Two workers in

navy blue coveralls came running across the street.

Nancy walked behind the car and saw that George was right. The chess piece was a knight. A larger-than-life cloaked rider, sword upraised, sat astride a horse that didn't look too powerful at the moment. The horse had rolled across the street, hit the curb, and pitched forward, nose in the grass.

While one worker ran to the horse, the other jogged up to Nancy and gently put a hand on her arm. "Are you okay? I was loading the chess piece onto the dolly to bring it down the truck ramp, but it got away from me."

Nancy noticed that the man was only a few years older than she was. He was tall, with bright, intelligent blue eyes and tousled dark hair. He had a deep tan—from working outside, Nancy guessed.

"We're fine," she replied. "I thought we were back in medieval times there for a second. You know, knights on horseback and all that."

"I didn't mean to scare you," the man said. "My name's Christopher Hurley, and you are?"

"Nancy Drew," Nancy said, shaking his hand.

Donna strode over from the other side of the car and angrily stuck her finger in the worker's chest. "Chris Hurley! You did that on purpose!"

Nancy stepped back, startled. Donna and Chris obviously knew each other.

George and Danitra came over.

"You tell him, Donna," Danitra said.

Chris didn't answer Donna. He looked at her, but talked to Nancy. "I'm really sorry. You have no idea how relieved I am that nobody got hurt."

Nancy noticed that the other worker, who had his long brown hair pulled back in a tight ponytail, had the horse and rider upright again. They didn't seem to be damaged. "I'm sure it was an accident," she said.

"I hope so," the worker said as he pushed the game piece back across the street on its wooden casters. "Be more careful from now on, Hurley."

Chris nodded. He looked at Nancy as if he had something else to say.

Donna didn't give him a chance. "Come on," she said to Nancy, then spun back. "I'm playing in this chess tournament, Coach Hurley. So don't try to stop me!"

"I'll get you to change your mind, Donna," Chris said calmly. "You'll see."

Nancy was completely confused. Once they were all in the car, she started the engine and pulled away, watching Chris Hurley in her mirror. He stood there, still as a statue, disappearing from view when Nancy rounded a corner.

"What was that all about?" George asked.

Donna took a deep breath. "I'm sorry. He just makes me so mad sometimes I can barely talk about it."

"I can!" Danitra said. "That guy is a track coach at Evanston College in Chicago. He keeps trying to get Donna to quit chess and spend her time running at Evanston when she graduates from high school. He's been offering her a scholarship for the past two years."

"So what's he doing with a job here at the tournament?" George asked.

Donna picked up the leather chess case from the floor, then smoothed her skirt. "He'll do anything to let me know he thinks chess is a waste of time."

"He turns up at every tournament," Danitra added.

"There are five or six college track coaches trying to get me to quit chess and run for them when I'm done with high school," Donna said, looking at Nancy. "They write letters, and even phone my parents all the time. Don't be surprised if one of them calls your house while I'm here."

"Don't worry," Nancy said, turning onto her street. "You'll have complete privacy this week. I can talk to the tournament officials if you want. We can report what just happened."

"No, it's all right," Donna said. "I'd rather not make a big deal about it. Coach Hurley's not a bad person. He's just intense about running." She brightened. "Was the huge outdoor chess set what you wanted to show me?"

Nancy nodded. "We'll get a closer look tonight at the opening ceremony."

"Great!" Danitra said. "Hey, Donna, show Nancy and George the set Grandpa gave you."

Donna turned in her seat so Danitra could see her hands. She moved her right hand in a circle in front of her chest, then made a fist and pushed it toward Danitra, ending with her index finger pointing up.

"Okay," Danitra said.

"I think I missed something," George said.

"American Sign Language?" Nancy asked as she pulled into her driveway.

Donna smiled. "Right, Nancy. I just told Danitra to relax and give me a minute. Our mother works at a school for the deaf, and sign language comes in handy sometimes."

"Especially at chess tournaments," Danitra said. "My mom and I can talk to each other while we watch and not disturb the players."

The girls grabbed the Winstons' luggage and headed into Nancy's house. Inside, they dropped the bags in the hall and settled in the living room.

Donna and Nancy sat on the couch. While Donna carefully placed the leather case on the glass-topped coffee table, George and Danitra pulled up chairs.

"As I said, my grandfather gave this to me." Donna unzipped the case and pulled out a beautiful antique chess set. The board was made of dark mahogany inlaid with smooth, polished squares of onyx and ivory.

"Oh, wow, it's amazing," Nancy said. "Set it up for us."

Donna turned the board over. Unlatching a false bottom, she revealed a velvet-lined compartment. Each of the chess pieces lay in its own form-fitting cell.

Donna pulled pieces out several at a time and handed them to the other girls to hold. Then she set the board on the table.

"These are different from the pieces on the big outdoor board," George said. She held up a small elephant carved out of dark blue marble and a tiny whitish yellow marble chariot.

Donna nodded. "Most people think chess started in India," she said. "These chessmen represent the four parts of the Indian army—elephants, horses, chariots, and foot soldiers."

The girls placed the pieces on their proper squares on the board. The dark king and queen faced the light king and queen from opposite sides of the board. Placed on the squares to either side of them, like bookends, were the matching elephants, then the horses, then, on the outside, the chariots. The eight pawns in each army covered the row just in front of the other pieces.

"So," Nancy said, "the elephants in your game

are the same as the bishops on a regular board, and the horses look pretty much the same as knights."

"Exactly," Donna said. "And instead of little castles, the rooks on my board are chariots."

"I think Donna's board makes it easier to remember how the pieces move," Danitra said.

"How so?" George asked.

Danitra moved one of the little soldiers forward one square. "Well, the pawns are like real soldiers. They move slowly, one or two squares at a time."

"But elephants and chariots are faster," Donna added. She picked up an elephant. "A bishop moves diagonally across the board as long as no other pieces are in its way." She placed the elephant back on the board and picked up a chariot. "And rooks can move as far as they want in a straight line."

"What about the knights?" George asked.

"They're the most complicated," Donna said. "Think of horses as being more agile than bishops or rooks." She placed her hand on one of the dark blue horses and made it jump over the pawn sitting on the square in front of it. "The knight moves in an L shape. Two squares in one direction, and one more at a right angle."

"It's the only piece that can jump over other pieces," Danitra added. "The queen can't even do that, even though she's the most powerful piece in the game."

"She can go diagonally or straight, like a rook and a bishop," Nancy noted.

Donna nodded. "You capture the other player's piece when you can move one of your chessmen to a space it's on."

She set up an example, placing a yellow pawn on a square close to the center of the board. She then put one of the dark blue chariots three spaces away on the same row. "See, the blue rook can capture the yellow pawn because the rook can travel in a straight line and the pawn is on a space directly ahead of the rook."

"The idea is to capture your opponent's king," Danitra added. "You want to trap him so there's no way he can escape."

"But the king's so weak," Nancy said with a laugh. "He can only move one space in any direction."

Donna nodded. "That's why you have to protect him all the time."

"I can't wait to watch you play," George said. "Do you use this set?"

"No," Donna replied. "In tournaments you play with sets they provide. I practice with this set—it's my good luck charm."

"She takes it everywhere she goes," Danitra said.

A knock on the front door interrupted their conversation.

"That must be Bess and Anna," Nancy said, getting up.

Sure enough, when Nancy opened the door, George's cousin Bess and another girl stepped into the living room.

"This is Bess Marvin and Anna van Leeuwen," Nancy said, introducing the two girls to the Winstons.

Bess was a few inches shorter than her cousin, and her long blond hair contrasted with George's short dark curls. "Anna and I couldn't wait to meet you, Donna," she said as she sat down in an armchair facing the couch.

Danitra sat next to Anna. "So you're Anna van Leeuwen. You must be related to Greta van Leeuwen, the other top-ranked player in the tournament."

Anna laughed. She was small and slender, with shoulder-length auburn hair. "Yes. She's my older sister." Anna was from the Netherlands, but her English was perfect.

"Did you come all the way from Europe to watch your sister compete?" Donna asked.

"Oh, I've been in River Heights for the past year," Anna said.

"Anna's an exchange student at the high school," Bess explained. "She's staying with the Codys, a family down the street."

"That's fantastic," Donna said. "Do you like it here?"

"I love it!" Anna said. "I played point guard on the basketball team, and I've made lots of friends here. Too bad my sister hates it so much."

Nancy brought in a chair from the dining room and sat down. "Why is Greta unhappy?"

"She and my brother, Eric, have been doing an exhibition tour here in the U.S. for the past three weeks," Anna answered. "She keeps saying she's homesick and wants to leave. I think she misses our parents."

"They didn't come with her?" George asked.

Anna tilted her head to the side. "They don't like to fly," she said. "They take the train to all her matches in Europe, but they stayed home this time."

"That's too bad," George said.

Anna nodded. "This is Greta's first big tournament in this country. I wish she could be more excited about it."

"Greta and I have never played each other," Donna said. "I'm looking forward to that match."

"So am I, Donna," Danitra said. "I get bored watching you kill all your opponents."

The girls all laughed.

"Are you ready to continue the lesson?" Bess asked as she and Anna got up to leave.

Anna nodded. She pulled a set of keys from the

pocket of her soccer shorts. "Bess is teaching me how to drive."

"Yes. I'm afraid my poor car is doomed," Bess said.

Anna giggled. "I guess I do like to go a little bit fast." She turned to Danitra. "Want to come with us?"

"Sounds like fun," Danitra said. "I think I'm brave enough, and I'd like to know how *you* feel about being the little sister of a chess genius."

George decided to catch a ride home with Bess, Anna, and Danitra.

Once the other girls had left, Nancy sat down next to Donna.

"Danitra and Anna hit it off well," she said.

"I'm glad," Donna said. "Danitra always wants to come with me to these tournaments, but sometimes she gets lonely when I'm practicing all the time."

Nancy was about to show Donna to her bedroom when the phone rang. "Excuse me," she said as she jogged into the kitchen to pick up the receiver. She could hardly hear the voice at the other end of the line because there was so much static.

"Hello. This is Norris Stricker. May I speak with Donna?"

"Yes, of course," Nancy said.

Nancy called for Donna and handed her the phone. "It's Coach Stricker."

As Donna listened, Nancy watched her expression go completely blank.

Nancy had a terrible thought. The voice sounded pretty much the way she remembered Stricker's voice sounding. But what if it wasn't Mr. Stricker? she thought. It might be Coach Hurley—and I promised Donna only a little while ago that she'd have total privacy.

Donna hung up the phone without saying anything. Her expression told Nancy that the news was not good.

"That wasn't your coach, was it?" Nancy asked.

"No," Donna mumbled. She sat down heavily in one of the kitchen chairs and looked up at Nancy.

"I don't know who that was," Donna said. "But he told me to lose in the first round of the tournament or else . . ." Her voice trailed off.

"Or else what?"

"He said if I didn't lose, it would be the last game I ever played."

# 3

## *Grand Master Mismatch*

Nancy took Donna's hand to comfort her. "Did you recognize the voice?" she asked.

Donna shook her head slowly. "It sounded far away, kind of muffled and scratchy," she said. "Like maybe he put a handkerchief or something over the mouthpiece."

"Did he say anything else?"

Again Donna shook her head. Putting her hands on her cheeks, she closed her eyes and took a deep breath to calm herself. "He said, 'This isn't your game, Donna' in a really scary-sounding voice. Then he told me to drop out of the tournament now or lose in the first round."

"Are you sure it wasn't Chris Hurley?"

"I don't think Coach Hurley would do something this mean," Donna said. "He wants me to quit chess, but it doesn't do him any good if I get so mad at him that I go to college somewhere else."

"But what if he figures you'll never find out it was him?" Nancy asked.

Donna clenched her fists. "Oh, I don't know. It could've been anyone."

Nancy stood up and reached for the phone. "Should we call your parents?"

Donna jumped up quickly. "No. This is probably nothing. I don't want to disturb my dad while he's in the middle of a case, and my mom's in California at a conference." She pulled Nancy's hand from the receiver. "I don't want to worry them."

"What if we call the tournament officials?" Nancy suggested.

"Let's wait to see if anything else happens." Donna paced back and forth next to the kitchen counter. "I'm sure it's only somebody's idea of a joke."

Though she was skeptical, Nancy finally agreed.

Managing a thin smile, Donna said, "Let me change my clothes. Then can you take me on a tour of River Heights?"

"Great idea," Nancy said.

A few minutes later Donna came back downstairs dressed in khaki pants and a blazer.

Nancy pulled her shoulder-length strawberry blond hair back into a ponytail. "We'll go to the convention center first," she said. "That way you can get a look at where you'll be playing."

It was just past eleven in the morning, and traffic was much lighter now. Nancy made it downtown in no time.

The two girls parked in a bank parking lot across the street from the River Heights Convention Center and headed for the main entrance.

The center sprawled right up to the edge of the cement flood wall of the Muskoka River; it was designed to resemble the huge riverboats that had steamed up the river a hundred years earlier.

The first two stories of the building had very few windows, giving the impression of the flat, bargelike structure of an old paddleboat.

The next three stories grew progressively smaller. They were constructed mostly of glass rather than brick, so they would look like the upper passenger decks. Two clock towers rose from the roof like smokestacks.

Inside, it was cool and dimly lit, and Nancy and Donna had to wait a few seconds for their eyes to adjust.

"This is nice," Donna said, noting the marble floor of the entrance hall. "Is that where the chess tournament is being held?" she asked, pointing to a row of doors off to their right.

Nancy led the way. A sign over the doors read: Exposition Room C. There seemed to be a bustle of activity inside.

No sooner did Nancy stick her head through one of the doors than she felt someone grab her arm and pull her forward.

"Hey! What's—?"

"Finally!" a man's voice said loudly. "You took your time getting here, princess!"

Nancy almost stumbled to the floor. She found herself standing in front of a tall, thin man wearing black dress slacks and a gray turtleneck.

"You've got ten minutes to get dressed, young lady. Let's go now, quick—quick." The man clapped his hands twice.

Nancy looked behind her. "Oh, now I get it," she said. She saw a long runway set up in the middle of the cavernous room. A glittering sign hung from the ceiling: A Night Under the Stars: The Spring Collection of Pierre Malhonette.

"I'm not a model," Nancy said. She glanced at Donna, who'd just stepped into the room behind her. "We're looking for the chess tournament."

The man kept staring. "Not a model. I don't believe it." He turned to Donna, taking her in from head to toe. "And you! You're perfect—the two of you are perfect!"

He pointed an index finger at each of them. "Forget about chess, girls. I'll pay you each loads of money to model my collection this weekend."

Donna held her hands up and laughed. "Sorry."

Nancy politely declined as well. As they left the room and walked down the hall, Nancy and Donna grinned at each other. They passed a room filled with different brands of shiny motorcycles, many of them painted with wild designs.

"It must be upstairs," Nancy said.

Together, they trotted up a broad staircase to the second level of exhibition halls.

The second floor was busier than the first. Light streamed in through the windows, and animal cages were stacked against a wall.

"Well, it isn't in there," Nancy said, pointing to a sign. "It's a dog show."

"This way," Donna said.

Around the corner, they came to the main hall. "We found it," Nancy said.

Exhibition Hall A was like the grand ballroom in a fantastic European hotel. The room was at least a hundred and fifty feet long, and dazzling brass chandeliers hung from the two-story ceiling. Lush carpet with repeating chess-piece designs had obviously been laid just for the tournament.

Nancy and Donna stepped in. "There must be over fifty chess sets," Nancy mumbled.

"Sixty-four, to be exact," Donna said.

Long conference tables were set up in the center of the room, and workers were pairing up chairs to face each other across the tables. Rows of plain, wooden chess sets sat on the tables, a little clock with two faces next to each one.

"What are those odd-looking clocks?" Nancy asked.

Donna went over to the nearest one and pushed a button. The second hand started moving on one of the clock's faces. Donna pushed another button and it stopped.

"There's a time limit," Donna explained. "When you make a move, you hit the button on your side. It starts the other player's clock. After your opponent moves, she hits the button, stopping her clock and starting yours.

"In early rounds you get an hour to make your first forty moves, then fifty minutes to finish the game," she continued. "If you get to the semifinals you get more time."

Nancy wanted to ask more questions, but at that moment a woman strode up to them and put a hand on Donna's shoulder.

"Donna Winston," she said. "How are you, dear?"

"Esther!" Donna said. She motioned to Nancy. "This is my friend Nancy Drew," Donna said. "Nancy, this is Esther Illatavy, World Chess Champion and director of this tournament."

"*Ex*-champion," Esther corrected. She smiled at Nancy. "I retired from competition two years ago to help promote chess in the United States.

We need to get more young women like Donna interested in our game."

Esther looked more like a basketball coach than a chess champion to Nancy. She wore a linen pantsuit and was easily an inch or two taller than Donna. Her thick, graying hair was brushed straight back from her forehead and trimmed at the ends so it curled at her collar. Her pale blue eyes bored right into Nancy. "Do you play, Miss Drew?"

"Not really," Nancy replied. "But Donna's teaching me a few things."

"Good." Esther turned back to Donna. "We must make the most of this week," she said. "You and Greta are the highest-ranked young women in the world. We're going to have expert commentators, videotapes of all the important matches. . . ." She motioned to a camera and microphone suspended above a square table at the center of the room. "I want to see you and Greta facing each other at that table at the end of the week. Two young women in the final match would be fantastic for us all."

Donna nodded solemnly.

Esther crossed her arms and leaned in close to Nancy and Donna, as if letting them in on a secret. "Are you listening to me, Donna?"

Donna nodded again, but Nancy wondered what Esther was really getting at.

"Try to get to know Greta over the next few days," Esther said. She placed a hand on Donna's shoulder. "Greta's talking about going back to Europe right after this tournament. If we can get her to stick around for a few more months, say, to develop a nice rivalry with you, we could get a lot of good press out of it."

"You want us to be friends?" Donna asked.

"No, no, dear. The opposite, actually. I think she's losing her competitive spirit. The two of you vying at every tournament for top ranking might get her excited again."

Esther trained her hard gaze on Donna. She seemed to see what she wanted and gave the young player a pat on the shoulder. "I've got to get ready for the press conference," she said. "I'll see you later, I'm sure."

When she was gone, Donna frowned at Nancy. "As if I didn't have enough pressure on me already."

"I'll say." Nancy sighed. "She was a bit much."

Donna threw her hands in the air. "Whatever," she said, starting for the door. "Why don't we continue our River Heights tour at your favorite lunch place? It'll be my treat."

"That's the kind of tour I love to lead," Nancy said. "Follow me."

After lunch the girls stopped off at Nancy's

house to pick up Donna's chess set. Then Nancy dropped her off at the Ambassador Hotel downtown so she could go over her strategy with Coach Stricker.

They made plans to find each other again at the opening ceremonies that night.

That evening Nancy's father, Carson Drew, came home to eat dinner with Nancy, Danitra, and Hannah Gruen, the Drews' housekeeper. Donna had already left for a final meeting with Coach Stricker before the opening ceremonies.

"I've got to go back to the office for a while," Mr. Drew said as they finished up their dessert.

He turned to Danitra. "Your dad called me this afternoon. He may need help on this case he's working on."

"Wow," Danitra said. "It must be a really big deal."

Mr. Drew nodded. "I might have to go up to Chicago. We'll see."

"Are you going to make it to the news conference after the ceremony, Dad?" Nancy asked.

"I'll be there," Mr. Drew said. He smiled. "Save me a seat, will you?"

"No problem," Nancy answered as she got up to help Hannah with the dishes.

Forty-five minutes later, at around seven P.M., she and Danitra found Donna and Norris Stricker in the bleachers in Riverside Park.

"What a great turnout," Nancy said as everyone sat down.

The sun was setting behind the river, and temporary spotlights had been set up to illuminate the giant chess set. The pieces stood at attention in the long shadows of the trees like soldiers ready to do battle.

"This should be exciting," Coach Stricker said as he opened his glossy program. "It says here that Esther Illatavy and Josip Armand are going to play a match using this life-size chess set."

Nancy now had the chance to see the set up close for the first time. The pieces looked ancient. The bishops wore the traditional pointed miter—almost like a little church spire—on their heads. The queens and kings each wore a crown and a long cloak. The kings had little goatees, as well.

"The pawns don't look like normal pawns," Danitra said, echoing Nancy's thoughts. "They look like gravestones."

Nancy nodded. "Eerie."

"It's a replica of the Lewis chess set," Donna explained. "Pieces just like these were found on an island a long time ago. They're some of the most famous ancient chess pieces. They look pretty scary, don't you think?"

Nancy nodded.

The girls spotted Bess, George, and Anna van Leeuwen sitting in the bleachers on the opposite

31

side of the chessboard. They waved, and Nancy noticed a girl who looked very much like Anna, except with glasses, sitting with them.

"That must be Anna's sister, Greta," Nancy said.

"Yes, that's her," Donna said. "I've seen pictures of her in chess magazines."

"Should we go sit with them?" Danitra asked.

Before Nancy could answer, a voice boomed over an intercom system: "Welcome, chess players and chess fans, to the International Junior Masters Chess Championship!"

A cheer went up from the crowd.

"Too late to move," Donna said.

"Please help me welcome the former world champion, Esther Illatavy!" the announcer said.

The crowd clapped wildly as she climbed up the steps of a platform behind the white chess pieces.

The announcer then introduced Josip, an older, stoop-shouldered man who waved as he climbed to his position behind the black chessmen.

"How are they going to move the huge chess pieces from there?" Nancy asked.

Her question was answered when Esther called her first move into her microphone. "Queen's pawn. D2 to D4," she said.

"D2 to D4 is chess notation," Donna whispered. "The columns on a board are lettered **A** through **H** and the rows are numbered one through eight, like a graph. So, it's kind of a shorthand to let people know what the moves are."

The crowd was silent. A figure wearing a black, hooded cape stepped out from the shadows under the platform.

Danitra was on the edge of her seat. "That looks like somebody dressed in a spooky Halloween costume," she whispered.

The cloaked figure pushed the pawn in front of the white queen up two squares, then retreated into the shadows again.

"Queen's knight," Josip said quickly. "B8 to C6."

A matching figure stepped out from under Josip's podium and pushed a knight up two spaces and over one.

"King's pawn," Esther said. "E2 to E3." The pawn in front of Esther's king advanced one space.

Josip followed by moving up the pawn that was in front of his queen.

Esther then ordered her assistant to push the bishop next to her king diagonally across the board until it stopped one diagonal space away from the knight Josip had moved out.

"Oohs" and "aahs" went up from the crowd.

"What's happening?" Nancy whispered.

Donna leaned over. "She could take his knight with her bishop. He's got to move it."

"C6 to B4," Josip said.

"Yup," Donna said. "He's getting it out of the way."

The crowd murmured as Josip's cloaked helper came out and headed not for the knight, but for the queen. The figure pushed the black queen up two spaces, next to the knight.

Josip cleared his throat. "That's not the move I wanted. I asked to move my knight."

Esther's assistant stepped out onto the center of the board and shouted something.

People in the crowd were standing now. Esther Illatavy had a shocked expression on her face.

Josip's assistant shook a fist at the crowd, then raced over and slammed the other cloaked figure roughly to the ground.

"What on earth—" Norris Stricker cried.

Josip's assistant smashed into Esther's row of pawns, knocking them over like dominoes.

"Why is he ruining the game?" Danitra cried.

# 4

# *Captured!*

"Stop it!" Esther shrieked into the microphone. "Stop this man immediately!"

The figure charged at the white king like a football player. The heavy king rocked back on its base, but didn't fall.

Tournament officials in red vests ran onto the painted chessboard. One of them grabbed a piece of the cape, but the dark figure twisted free and darted to the far side of the board.

"Who is that?" Danitra said.

"He's fast, whoever he is," Nancy replied. She jumped out of the stands to get a better view.

The hooded person was making fools of the tournament officials, running in between and around all the chess pieces as he was chased.

From up on the platform, Josip called out, "Someone call the police, please."

Nancy felt Donna jump down beside her. Without a word, they both ran under the lights and onto the grassy chessboard.

Nancy headed to the left, while Donna circled around from the right.

The culprit was at the far side of the board. An official dived for him, but the figure easily skipped free.

Nancy slowly crept between the two rows of black pieces; the short, stumpy pawns on her right, and the major pieces towering over her left shoulder.

As she peeked over a pawn, she saw the figure freeze. He'd just spotted Donna closing in on him. He whirled and sprinted straight for Nancy's side of the board.

In a flash Nancy reacted. She couldn't let this person escape past her into the night. The piece next to her was the bishop. She pushed it with all her strength.

The heavy wooden figure tilted precariously— then toppled. The cloaked man tried to leap over it, but wasn't nimble enough.

He tripped and fell to the ground.

The crowd cheered.

In seconds Nancy, Donna, and the three officials had surrounded the culprit. "Way to go!" someone shouted.

Nancy reached down and pulled back the hood of the black cloak.

"I recognize you!" she said. It was the ponytailed worker who'd been helping Chris Hurley unload the chess pieces. "Who are you?"

The man said nothing.

"Gary Kempton," one of the officials answered for him. "You're in big trouble, buddy."

Two burly police officers showed up and dragged Gary to his feet.

"Hey, man! This wasn't my idea," Gary protested.

"Save it," an officer said as he clamped a pair of cuffs on Kempton's wrists.

"No, let him talk," one of the officials said. "I would like to hear whose idea it was, Gary!"

"I got a message this afternoon," Kempton began. "Some guy said he'd leave me the cloak and an envelope with two hundred bucks under that podium there."

"His name?"

"He didn't say; I didn't ask. He told me to mess up the game, tackle the other dude, then take off. I thought it was a joke, man. I'm sorry."

"It was a very poor joke," the official said.

"If that's what it was," Nancy said. She scanned the park. "Whoever the other cloaked figure was, he's long gone now."

She and Donna headed back to the stands.

"That was incredible," Danitra said when they

got back to their seats. "Professional wrestling and chess all in one."

Donna laughed, but Nancy could tell that she was concerned.

"I'm wondering if there's some connection to the phone call you got this afternoon," Nancy whispered.

"I don't know," Donna said. "Now I'm hoping it was Chris Hurley's sick idea of a prank and not something more serious."

Nancy nodded. "I'll have to find out who hired Kempton."

After tournament officials got the crowd quieted down, they asked for two new volunteers to help out with the match—this time without wearing cloaks.

Esther and Josip turned out to be good sports about the whole thing. They played a lively match, and Esther finally won, trapping Josip's king in a corner of the board.

The crowd stood to applaud the two Grand Masters.

"That was fantastic," Norris said. "You could be that great, Donna, if you wanted to."

The announcer then invited the press into the convention center media room to meet the top players.

"Time to go perform," Donna said. She and Norris followed a group of reporters, including

Brenda Carlton, to a back entrance of the building.

Nancy, Danitra, and other members of the crowd followed the officials' directions through the front.

The media room turned out to be in the basement of the convention center. It was a narrow, brightly lit, windowless room with a long dais set up at the far end.

Padded folding chairs were set up in rows facing the dais, with several spaces left clear for cameras to be set up to shoot at different angles.

Nancy and Danitra found Mr. Drew, George, and Bess at the door, and they all filed in together.

"Bess says I missed some excitement," Nancy's father said.

"Nancy was awesome!" Danitra said, quickly filling Carson Drew in on the turmoil during the match.

Mr. Drew shook his head. "Some people will do anything to draw attention to themselves."

"Seriously," George agreed. "We couldn't believe it."

They found a row of seats together and sat down. "I don't know," Bess said. "Anna was angry about it, but Greta seemed to think it was pretty funny."

Nancy hoped it was just a simple prank, but

she feared it was more serious than that. She thought about telling her father about the phone call but decided against it. Now wasn't the right time.

"Save a seat for Anna," Bess told George. "She wanted to talk to her sister before the press conference, but she said she'd be here in a few minutes."

George nodded, then placed her program on the empty seat next to her.

Danitra told Nancy about the driving lesson Anna had had that afternoon while they waited for the press conference to begin.

"I thought we were going to be playing harps three or four times," Danitra said. "We just missed getting into some major accidents."

Bess had her compact out and was checking her makeup. "Anna must have a guardian angel," she said with a smile.

Five, then ten minutes passed. Finally a door behind the dais opened, and Esther Illatavy stepped into the room. The top-ranked participants followed her and took seats at the long table.

Donna and Norris Stricker sat on one side of the podium, while a slender blond girl with blue-framed glasses sat on the other side.

"That's Greta van Leeuwen," Bess whispered to Nancy.

"Yes," Nancy said. "I saw her sitting with you in the bleachers. How old is she?"

"Seventeen—a year older than Anna," Bess said. "Ooh, look! There's her brother, Eric. Isn't he cute?"

"He is handsome," Nancy admitted.

Eric sat down next to Greta at the table. He appeared to be eighteen or nineteen years old and was tall, with wavy blond hair and broad shoulders. He had a green baseball cap tilted back on his head.

Nancy recognized a few of the other players at the table. The seven-year-old girl she'd seen at the bus station carrying the teddy bear was there with her mother. And four boys, ranging in age from twelve or thirteen to late teens, also had places at the table of honor.

Nancy noticed that Greta and Eric were having what looked like an argument. Eric had his hand over the microphone in front of them.

Greta said one final thing, then turned away. Her brother tried to say something else, but Greta ignored him.

Esther Illatavy went to the podium and introduced the players and their coaches, then opened the floor to questions.

A reporter from a local television station stood up and asked Donna if she had a special strategy worked out for this tournament.

Donna leaned toward her microphone, but Coach Stricker jumped in before she could say anything.

"Donna has a tendency to lay back, to play a more intellectual type of game," Stricker said. "As her coach, I'm working with her to pick the right moments to be more aggressive."

The reporter seemed annoyed that Donna hadn't responded to the question. "Do you consider yourself a passive player?" he asked.

"No. I think I—"

Again Stricker jumped in. Rather than answer the question, he spoke about different styles of chess.

Bess turned to Nancy with a concerned expression on her face. "I wonder where Anna is?" she whispered. "She was supposed to meet us here."

Nancy looked around the room. "Maybe she's back in the press lounge waiting for her brother and sister to finish up here."

Bess nodded.

When Coach Stricker was done, Brenda Carlton jumped up. "Greta, there's a rumor that you hate the United States. Is that true?"

Greta's face reddened. At first Nancy thought it was just a blush from embarrassment, but then it seemed that Greta was on the verge of tears.

"No. I don't hate the United States," Greta said, her voice little more than a whisper. "I'm just homesick. Some people want me to stay here." Greta glanced at her brother. "But I want to go home as soon as this tournament is over. I miss my parents."

"Who wants you to stay?" Brenda asked. "Eric? You're acting as Greta's coach—do you want her to stay?"

Eric nodded. "I like it here," he said. "We've been here for three weeks, touring and playing exhibition matches. My sister Anna has been here for a year as an exchange student. She loves it, too."

"But why should Greta stay if she hates it?"

Eric's face hardened. He seemed annoyed. "Even though chess isn't as popular here as it is in the Netherlands," he said, "there's a lot more money here. I think Greta could make a lot of money if she stayed, if she just gave it more of a chance."

Someone else stood up. "Who's the better chess player, Greta—you or your brother?"

The crowd laughed.

Greta managed a smile, but it seemed forced to Nancy.

"Eric taught me to play when we were both little," she said with a shrug. "He used to beat me all the time."

Eric put an arm around his sister and grinned. "I haven't won against her since she was ten years old," he said.

The crowd laughed again.

After a few more questions, Esther ended the conference and invited everyone back to watch the start of the tournament the next day.

Nancy's group went out into the hallway to wait for Donna to come out of the press lounge. When Donna and Norris came out, Mr. Drew had news for everyone.

"Donna, your father called me again," he said. "He needs me to go to Chicago for a few days to help with his case. I'll be leaving early in the morning, but Hannah will be home, of course," he said.

"It must be a real emergency," Danitra said.

Mr. Drew nodded. "The good news is that he thinks we'll be done in time to get back for the finals Saturday evening."

"Oh, I hope so," Donna said. "It'd be great if he could be here."

Mr. Drew offered to give Coach Stricker a ride back to his hotel.

Stricker gladly accepted, and Nancy gave her dad a quick hug, telling him they'd see him at home.

"Your coach doesn't let you do much talking, does he?" George said when the hallway had cleared.

"He thinks he's destined to be some great chess promoter," Donna said. "I let him talk—it's no big deal."

Nancy saw Greta van Leeuwen step out of the press lounge and look up and down the hallway.

The Dutch player spotted Bess and trotted

44

over. Up close, it looked to Nancy as if Greta had been crying.

"Bess," she said, taking Bess's hand. "You're such a good friend to Anna. Can I talk to you—in private?"

Bess nodded, puzzled. She and Greta walked down the hall, out of earshot.

Nancy watched as Greta showed something to Bess and then broke down in tears. They talked for a few minutes, then Bess walked back over to Nancy, her face pale.

Her hand shaking, Bess handed Nancy a folded slip of paper.

Nancy opened it.

Bold block letters said:

GRETA VAN LEEUWEN—I HAVE YOUR SISTER. SHE IS SAFE AND UNHARMED— FOR NOW. IF YOU TELL THE POLICE— OR ANYONE ELSE—THAT SHE IS MISS- ING, YOU WILL NEVER SEE HER AGAIN. I WILL CONTACT YOU SOON WITH FUR- THER INSTRUCTIONS.

# 5

## Two Dead Kings

Nancy's mind raced. Anna—kidnapped! She quickly folded the note.

"What's up?" Donna asked.

Nancy stuck the note in the pocket of her shorts. "Greta and Eric are having some problems with their hotel reservations," she said. "Bess and I will go over to help straighten things out."

Nancy felt bad about lying to Donna about what was going on, but whoever had written the note had been very clear: no one was to know. Nancy didn't want to put Anna in further danger.

Nancy asked George to take Donna and Danitra home.

Bess handed George her car keys.

"Donna, can you tell my dad I'll be home soon?" Nancy asked.

"No problem," Donna said. She smiled. "Your dad asked for a chess lesson. I figure now's a good time to show him what's what."

Nancy laughed. "Go easy on him."

When the others had gone, Nancy and Bess returned to Greta's side.

Nancy introduced herself to Greta and surveyed the hallway. She didn't want anyone to overhear their conversation.

A few people were still milling around. Nancy saw Brenda Carlton packing her camera away right outside the conference room door.

Brenda looked over at them.

Nancy smiled and waved. She nudged Bess and Greta. "Smile, you guys," she whispered. "Before she comes over here and starts asking questions."

Greta managed a weak wave.

"Come on," Nancy said. "We need privacy." She led the way out of the convention center and back into Riverside Park. It was close to ten-thirty now. The lights around the outdoor chess set had been turned off, but the moon was almost full and gave off a soft yellow glow.

Nancy, Bess, and Greta sat on a park bench facing the river. The water lapped quietly against the flood wall, and no one else seemed to be around.

"Okay," Nancy said calmly. "Tell us what happened."

Greta took her glasses off and dabbed at her eyes. "Eric found the note on my backpack."

"And before that," Nancy asked, "when did you last see Anna?"

"She was with us at the outdoor chess match," Greta said, her voice quavering. "I left early to meet Eric in the lounge."

Nancy asked, "What time exactly?"

"Before eight-thirty, I think. Somewhere around there. I went into the lounge, tossed my backpack down—"

"Who had access to it? Did you leave the lounge at all?" Nancy asked.

Greta nodded, tears rolling down her cheeks. "Anna said she'd come by to wish me luck before the press conference, but she never showed up. I kept leaving the lounge to look for her."

"You must know most of the other players," Nancy said. "Did you see anyone hanging around you didn't recognize?"

Greta pushed a strand of hair behind her ear. "It was crowded with kids, their parents, and many reporters. Anyone could've gotten in."

"When did Eric find the note?" Nancy asked.

"Right before Esther Illatavy led us out to the conference," Anna said. "She was late getting there."

Nancy leaned forward to look past Greta on the bench. "Bess, when did you last see Anna?"

A little of Bess's natural rosy color had come back, but she still was pale. "At about eight forty-five or so, when the match was over," Bess said. "George and I got up with Anna and started walking to the convention center. Anna took off. She said she was going to go wish Greta luck, then meet us in the press room. That's why I asked George to save a seat."

Nancy nodded. "The press conference started late, at a little after nine-thirty. That means the kidnapper grabbed Anna—"

Greta let out a moan.

"I'm sorry," Nancy said. "I'm just trying to put this together. The kidnapper, or kidnappers, had to get Anna and drop off the note without being detected somewhere between eight forty-five and nine-thirty."

"The park was crowded," Bess said. "How could Anna just disappear?"

Nancy jumped as a loud voice came booming across the park.

"Greta! What are you doing?"

The three girls turned at once. Nancy let out a relieved sigh as she saw Eric van Leeuwen running out of the darkness of the park. He jogged around to the front of the bench, holding what Nancy assumed was Greta's black backpack in one hand.

"What's going on, Greta?" Eric demanded. "You told them, didn't you?"

"Bess and Nancy are Anna's friends," Greta said. "I was so frightened, I had to tell someone."

Eric groaned. "The note said not to tell *any-one*," he practically shouted. "What if something happens to Anna? Whoever took her could be watching us right now."

"That's right," Nancy said. "So keep your voice down."

Eric acted embarrassed for a second, then was silent. He began to pace in front of the bench.

Greta sat on the edge of her seat, hugging herself. "Maybe we should call the police. They know more about this sort of thing than we do."

Eric raised a hand, palm out. "No. Absolutely not. It's too much of a risk. We don't even know what the kidnapper wants yet."

Nancy stared out at the slow-moving river. Had the ruckus at the chess match been a diversion to set Anna up? she wondered. Was the kidnapping related to the telephone threat Donna had received earlier in the day?

There was no way to tell. Maybe this new crisis had nothing to do with the chess tournament at all.

"I think Eric's right," Nancy said at last. "We'll wait until whoever did this contacts you again."

"Oh," Greta said sadly. "I wish we could find Anna right now and go back home."

Nancy stood up. "Go back to the hotel. When the kidnapper contacts you again, call me or Bess."

"We will," Greta said.

Eric didn't say anything. He helped Greta to her feet. The two of them walked back toward the convention center.

Bess and Nancy headed for Nancy's car.

"I'm so worried about Anna," Bess said as they drove through downtown. "Who would do something like this?"

"We'll find out," Nancy promised.

As Nancy dropped Bess off and drove home, she wasn't so sure. She could only hope that Anna was safe and unharmed, as the kidnapper had said.

When Nancy went downstairs for breakfast the next morning—the first day of the tournament— she felt as if she had a head made of solid wood. She hadn't slept a wink.

The first thing she noticed was Donna's chess set on the dining room table. Almost all the yellow pieces were still on the board, but most of the dark blue pieces were lined up neatly at the edge of the table.

Nancy could see that the yellow player had

checkmated the dark blue player with ease. The blue king was pinned against the last row. A bishop kept him from moving to the next black square over, and the yellow queen had him straight in her sights.

She stepped into the kitchen. Donna and Danitra were already up and dressed.

"Looks like you gave my dad a pretty harsh chess lesson," Nancy said with a chuckle.

Danitra took a drink of orange juice. "He lasted about ten seconds."

"Danitra," Donna scolded. "Honestly, Nancy, he played well. But after a couple of test games he asked me to play my hardest, so I did." She lifted her hands apologetically.

Nancy laughed. "I'm sure he'll recover."

Hannah Gruen stepped out of the pantry. The Drews' housekeeper moved around the kitchen efficiently, wiping a spill off the stovetop, then getting two eggs from the refrigerator.

"Sit down, Nancy," she said. "Have some breakfast. Your father's already gone to Chicago, and Donna has to get to the tournament."

As soon as Nancy sat down, her stomach clenched up at the memory of the previous night's events. She was determined to find Anna's kidnapper, but she couldn't let anyone know that anything was wrong.

"Ready for today's matches?" she asked Donna.

Donna closed her eyes, as if concentrating hard. "Yes," she said. She opened her wide brown eyes and smiled. "Take me to my victims."

Half an hour later Nancy and the Winston girls met Norris Stricker outside the entrance to the main exhibition hall.

Officials were taking tickets at the doors, but Stricker showed his pass and the four of them were ushered in.

There was much more activity than there had been the day before. The tournament tables were set up to form a line down the center of the room. Rows of chairs went all the way back to the walls on either side of the tables. Spectators were already filing in and sitting down.

Players paced nervously or stood talking quietly in small clusters.

Coach Stricker stepped over to a huge cork bulletin board where the morning's pairings were posted. "You're playing Brian Nadel first—on the center table," he said, scribbling some notes on a clipboard.

"The center table?" Nancy said. "Doesn't that mean you're going to be the featured match this morning, Donna?"

Donna nodded and flexed her fingers as if getting ready to play the piano. "It shouldn't take too long."

Stricker glared at her. "Don't get overconfident. Lay back in the beginning—see what he's got. Then attack, attack, attack!"

They continued to discuss strategy for a few minutes. Then Nancy saw a man walk over to a desk at the front of the room. With Esther Illatavy beaming proudly next to him, he welcomed everyone to the morning's matches, then ordered the players to take their places.

"And remember, spectators," he cautioned. "We must have absolute quiet at all times."

Nancy, Danitra, and Stricker took seats as a hush fell over the crowd. The only sound was the creaking of the wooden chairs as players scooted up to their boards.

The official held his arm up, watching the second hand of a clock on the wall approach twelve. At precisely ten o'clock, he lowered his arm. "Light pieces, start your clocks."

All the players with white pieces reached over in unison, started their game clocks, then made their first moves.

Nancy felt her heart begin to thump. She was surprised at how nervous she felt for all the players. The silence made the atmosphere tense.

"Take a look above the tables," Danitra whispered. "Look at those television cameras."

Nancy glanced up. Two cameras the size of shoeboxes were suspended on wires over the players' tables. The cameras pointed straight down and could zip silently along the wires, then stop, poised above any of the many chessboards.

Television monitors in various spots in the room showed the action on a particular board. Captions under the picture said who the players were and explained some of the action.

Nancy scanned the long tables. Donna and Greta were easy to spot. As the two top-ranked players in the tournament, they were playing their matches at the center table.

Donna's opponent, Brian Nadel, appeared to be about eighteen. He played cautiously. Every time he started to make a move—placing his hand on a piece, beginning to move it—Donna would make a face as if to say, "Are you sure you want to do that?" and he would take his hand away and reconsider.

"Is it fair for Donna to do that?" Nancy asked. "To make him worry about his moves?"

"Yes," Danitra whispered. "Lots of chess is about trying to psych out your opponent."

Stricker leaned over. "Gary Kasparov, the world champion, is a master of psychological warfare," he said. "He sometimes jumps up from the table and walks away during his opponent's turn."

Nancy watched as Donna's tactics continued to work. Soon she had captured both of Brian's knights and a bishop.

"She's destroying him," Danitra said.

"Yes, she's playing well," Stricker agreed. "I'll take this chance to scout out her next opponent. Ask Donna to call me later at the hotel, will you?" He got up and wandered off.

Nancy turned her attention to Greta's match. The Dutch player was obviously distracted. She fidgeted in her seat, glanced continually around the room, and gnawed at her fingernails. Nancy knew that she must be frantic about her little sister.

Her opponent was an eleven- or twelve-year-old boy with a short haircut and rimless glasses.

Nancy looked for Eric but couldn't find him. She wondered if he was back at the hotel waiting for a note or a call from the kidnapper.

Danitra clenched her fists. "Yes!" she said.

Nancy glanced over at the center table. An official was standing behind Donna's chair, signaling that she had won her match.

Donna and her opponent stood and shook hands. As Donna came over to where Nancy and Danitra were sitting, an official handed her several small rose bouquets. They were from fans, similar to ones thrown on the ice for skating stars.

Donna thanked the man.

"Chess groupies," she joked as she hugged her sister and sat down.

"Nice!" Nancy said. "Those are beautiful."

The girls stuck around awhile longer to watch,

then quietly started out to go to an early lunch. Nancy turned back at the door. Greta was still playing—and appeared to be very tense.

Nancy had tried to make eye contact with her all morning, desperate to know if Greta had heard anything. Nancy then figured that Greta would have found a way to let her know if the situation with Anna had changed.

By the time they made it back to Nancy's house, Donna was concentrating on her next match. "They'll get tougher each round," she said.

"You mean they can actually take longer than ten minutes?" Nancy asked.

Donna laughed, but she suddenly became silent as they walked through the front door and turned toward the dining room.

Nancy saw Donna's shoulders go slack.

A breeze made the drapes snap against the front window frame. Nancy followed Donna's gaze to the dining room table.

All the pieces from Donna's prized chess set were missing—except two.

The marble kings lay on the board like tiny corpses. A small kitchen knife rose up next to each one of them.

# 6

## A Secret Conversation

Donna was already standing next to the dining room table. She reached down and pulled out one of the knives. The tip had been wedged in a crack between an onyx and an ivory square.

"I can't believe it," Nancy said angrily. "Is the board damaged?"

"No," Donna said quietly. She set the kings upright on the table and removed the other knife.

As she picked up the mahogany board and turned it over to return the kings to their places, a slip of paper fluttered out of the compartment.

Nancy picked it up. The words were formed out of individual letters cut from magazine pages. She read the message out loud.

You were supposed to lose the first match! I promise—you'll be much richer if you lose. A word of advice: The skewer is a valuable and dangerous weapon.

Donna's lips were set in a tight, angry line. "I'm not going to let this creep intimidate me," she said evenly. "And if I find out who did this, I'm going to skewer *him* through the heart!"

"Who knows you have this special chess set?" Nancy asked.

"Almost no—" Donna started, then corrected herself. "I almost forgot. I've done two interviews for chess magazines. I talked about the set in both articles. That means thousands of people know I carry it with me."

Danitra put a hand on her sister's shoulder. "Don't worry, Don. We'll get the pieces back."

"At least we know how the thief got in," Nancy said. "The dining room window's open." Nancy went over and pulled the window back down. "It was a pretty bold move—prying open a front window in broad daylight."

"We know something else," Donna said. "Whoever did this knows something about chess."

"How can you tell?" Nancy asked.

"The note," Donna said. "What it says about the skewer. In chess, a skewer is when you force your opponent to move a piece, then capture one hidden behind it. It's a very effective move."

Nancy nodded. "We have someone who knows chess and who knew we'd be out this morning."

Danitra's usually confident expression had changed to concern. "Do you think we should call someone? The police, maybe?"

Donna sat down in a dining chair and ran her fingers over the smooth surface of her antique chessboard. She looked up at Nancy, and the two of them nodded at the same time.

As Nancy went to the phone, she heard Donna trying to comfort her little sister. "It's probably just Coach Hurley," she was saying. "And if it was, I promise I'm going to run track at Evanston's biggest rival. I'll help them crush Evanston at every track meet."

Nancy heard Danitra laugh. Then the police dispatcher came on the line. He said an officer would be right over.

When the officer arrived, Donna and Nancy took turns explaining what had happened, including the menacing phone call Donna had received the day before.

"I know you probably have more important things to do than track down some old chess set," Donna said.

The officer glanced up from taking notes. "I can tell it's important to you," he said, tilting his hat back on his head with the tip of his pen. "And we always take threats seriously. Were you two at that exhibition match last night? Sounds like someone went to a lot of trouble to disrupt things."

"It was total chaos," Nancy said, wondering if all the recent events were related. She considered telling the officer that Anna van Leeuwen was missing, but decided it would be safer not to.

The sound of a car pulling into the driveway interrupted their conversation.

Hannah came in a few seconds later with a sack of groceries in each arm.

"What happened?" she blurted out.

Nancy grabbed the bags out of her arms and led her into the kitchen.

Nancy explained while the two of them started making lunch. She knew from experience that a sure way to get Hannah to worry less was to get her into the kitchen and cooking.

By the time they came out with a tray of fruit and sandwiches, the officer had gone outside to ask the neighbors if they'd noticed anyone suspicious prowling around.

"Oh, my gosh!" Donna said, checking her watch. "I have to get back to get ready for my afternoon match."

"Grab some pears, Danitra, and I'll take you over," Hannah said, wrapping a napkin around a couple of sandwiches. She went into the kitchen and came out with two brown paper lunch bags. "Nancy, eat some lunch. You can meet us there."

Nancy smiled. "I will, Hannah." She carefully locked the door behind them as they left.

I'll go for a run, she said to herself. Running always helped her think. She grabbed an apple off the table. Upstairs in her room, she changed into shorts, a royal blue polo shirt, and running shoes.

Nancy picked up her phone. She wanted to see if Bess had talked to Greta since the previous night.

There was no dial tone.

Nancy felt a quick pang of fear. Why would the phone be out? she wondered. She'd called the police just a little while earlier, so the problem with the line must have just happened. Was the thief in the house?

She peered out at the street from her window. The police cruiser was gone. There was only one thing to do.

Padding silently from room to room, she searched the closets. She lifted her bedskirt. Nothing.

Downstairs, she headed through the kitchen to the basement steps. As she passed the phone, she heard a tiny voice coming from the receiver. She picked it up.

"If you'd like to make a call, please hang up and try again," a recorded voice said. Nancy laughed at herself. She must not have hung up the phone completely after calling the police.

Grabbing her car keys, Nancy started out the door.

The shrill ring of the phone stopped her in her tracks. She ran back and picked up. "Yes?"

"Nancy!"

It was Bess, sounding out of breath.

"Nancy," Bess repeated. "I've been trying to call you. The kidnapper sent Greta another note!"

"I'll be right over." Nancy slammed down the phone and ran to her car.

Bess and George were standing on the Marvins' front porch when Nancy screeched to a halt at the curb. She lowered the window. "Where's Greta now?" she shouted.

"Back at the convention center," Bess answered as the two cousins ran up to the Mustang.

"Get in!" Nancy called.

George climbed into the back. "Bess told me the situation with Anna."

"Good," Nancy said. "Now, what's the news?" She stepped on the gas, taking off almost before Bess could get the passenger door shut.

"Greta lost her match this morning," Bess said. "And the kidnapper is very upset."

"Oh, no," Nancy said.

George leaned forward and rested an elbow on each front seat back. "We got to the tournament right after you left. We saw everything."

"I don't know very much about chess," Bess added, "but it looked to me like she dumped the match."

63

George nodded. "She put her queen right out there for him to take. It was so obvious."

"She's out of the tournament?" Nancy asked.

"It's double elimination," George said. "So this afternoon she plays someone else who lost. Lose twice, *then* you're out."

"And that's not even the really awful part," Bess said, nervously twisting a button on her blouse. "George and I went over to talk to Greta and she acted almost relieved to have lost."

"Yes, but tell her what happened," George prompted.

"Then Esther Illatavy practically swoops over and grabs Greta by the arm. She starts yelling at her right in front of everyone. 'What are you doing?' she says. 'What about the plans we had? How could you be so stupid?' and lots of other pretty mean things."

Nancy swung the car past a bus and into the convention center lot.

"Then all of a sudden Esther turned really nice," Bess continued. "She said Greta must be under too much pressure and that she'd definitely come out of the loser's bracket to win it all. Then she smiled this big, fake smile and took off."

Nancy parked the car.

"Then an official came over. He told Greta somebody just left a message for her at the announcer's desk." Bess paused for a breath. "George and I walked over there with her. An

64

official handed her an envelope. It had a note from the kidnapper in it."

"It said that if Greta didn't win the tournament, she'd never see Anna again," George said.

Bess clenched her hands together. "Poor Greta almost fainted."

Nancy sat still, thinking. "Did either of you actually see the note? Was it handwritten?"

"I saw it," Bess said. "Yes, it was in big, block letters, just like the one from last night."

"Not cut-out magazine letters?"

"No. Why?"

Nancy told her friends about the threats Donna had received and how the note was made of cut-out letters.

Bess's jaw dropped. "Knives? That must've been so scary."

"It was," Nancy admitted. "But Donna didn't let it get to her."

"Do you think the same person is going after Donna and Greta?" George asked.

"I don't know," Nancy said. "But at least now we know what the kidnapper's ransom is: victory for Greta. Let's get inside and see how things are going."

The atmosphere in the main exhibition room was hushed and tense. Nancy spotted Norris Stricker making notes by the big bulletin board and went over to ask him how Donna was faring.

"Take a look for yourself," he said with a quick

grin. He gestured toward the spectator section on the far side of the vast room.

Nancy saw Donna sitting next to Danitra and Hannah and eating her sandwich.

"She won in twelve moves," Stricker said quietly. "She's really playing well, especially considering what happened at lunch."

"She told you about it?" Nancy asked.

Norris nodded. "Horrifying, to say the least. But I think we should be careful not to overreact. It was probably only a cruel prank."

"I'm not so sure."

"Oh, no, no, no," Stricker said, shaking his pen in Nancy's face. "Donna has to concentrate. We need to do our best not to make a big deal out of it."

Bess stared at the center table, a frown on her face. "How about Greta. I don't see her."

"I've been following her match," Stricker replied. "Since she lost, she's not at the center table anymore." He pointed to one of the long tables extending toward the back of the hall. "She's down there, third game from the end."

"Is she okay?" Bess asked. "I mean, is she playing well?"

"Much better than this morning," Stricker said. "I expect she'll have this game wrapped up soon."

"Whew." Bess let out an audible sigh. "That's good to hear."

Nancy shot a glance at Bess. She didn't want

66

her friend blurting out that Greta had to win because her sister had been kidnapped.

Stricker hadn't seemed to have noticed anything odd about the reaction.

"There's Eric," Bess said, acting as if everything was normal. "I'll go help cheer Greta on."

She excused herself and headed behind the rows of chairs to the back of the room.

Nancy was about to ask Stricker why he was so confident that the threats Donna had received were only a prank, when Esther Illatavy interrupted them.

"Coach, do you have a moment?"

Stricker nodded at George and Nancy and followed Esther out of the exhibition hall.

On a hunch, Nancy grabbed George by the arm and pulled her toward the exit. "Come with me," she said. "I want to hear what's going on with these two."

Staying back a safe distance, they followed Coach Stricker and Esther out the double doors and then downstairs to the first floor.

As they rounded a corner near a row of public phones, Nancy held up a hand, motioning for George to stop.

"They're standing in a little alcove next to the ticket window," she whispered.

"Can you hear what they're saying?"

Nancy shook her head. "Too far away."

The girls backtracked a few yards along the wall, coming to a doorway. It was the women's restroom.

"In here," Nancy whispered, leading the way. She knew what she was looking for—they'd have to have a little luck.

"There!" she said, pointing to a vent high over the sinks. "They're talking right on the other side of this wall. Boost me up there."

George gave Nancy a boost onto one of the sinks. "I hope no one comes in here. This would be pretty embarrassing, Nan."

"Shhh!" Nancy put an ear to the vent. At first she heard only a mechanical hum, but then two voices filtered through to her.

". . . your chance to make a big splash in the chess world," Esther was saying. "This tour could make you rich if we promote it right."

"My player's doing fine," Stricker was saying. "It's Greta who's the problem. The rumor is she lost on purpose this morning."

"She's young," Esther said. "She doesn't understand yet what she means to the game. Eric wants to stay. She'll change her mind."

"How can you be sure?" Stricker asked.

There was a long pause before Esther spoke again. "Let me worry about Greta. She'll make it to the finals. I'm working on a plan that will guarantee it."

# 7

# A Message Written in Blood

Nancy felt goose bumps rise on her arms. She remembered Esther trying to get Donna to start a rivalry with Greta. What are Esther and Coach Stricker planning? Nancy wondered.

She listened some more, but it was just small talk about the tournament.

"Call me at the hotel this evening. Room Five-sixteen," Esther was saying to Coach Stricker. "I'll have tomorrow's match pairings by then."

"Okay. Help me down," Nancy whispered.

George gave her a hand as she jumped off the sink.

"What'd you hear?"

"Norris Stricker and Esther are up to something," Nancy said. "And it sounds kind of shady, if you ask me."

The two friends left the bathroom, first making sure the outside hall was clear.

"They both definitely want Donna and Greta to make it to the finals," Nancy continued as they walked briskly back up to the main exhibition hall. "It seems like they want to organize a big chess tour with those two as the main attraction."

"No wonder Esther was so mad when Greta lost this morning," George said, her eyes narrowing. "I thought she was going to explode."

Nancy grabbed George's wrist to slow her down. "Esther promised Coach Stricker she could practically guarantee that Greta would get to the finals. But would she go so far as to kidnap Anna to make Greta play her best?"

"It depends on if there's enough money at stake," George said.

"That's true," Nancy agreed.

Once they got back to the second floor, Nancy and George stopped outside the room where the dog show was taking place. The applause from the crowd covered their conversation.

"How could Esther kidnap Anna?" George asked. "She was playing that exhibition match when Anna disappeared last night."

"She might have someone helping her," Nancy said, thinking out loud. "Remember, the press conference started late because it took Esther something like twenty minutes to get there after the match was over."

George nodded. "But why would Esther try to frighten Donna? If Coach Stricker and Esther want her to make it to the finals against Greta, then they obviously wouldn't be trying to scare her into losing."

"There could be some part of the plan we don't know," Nancy replied. "But we do know Esther's hotel room number. I think we need to sneak over there the first chance we get to see what we can find."

The two girls walked back to the chess tournament. As they approached the entrance, a blur of white flashed in front of Nancy.

Someone crashed into her, knocking her to the floor.

"Excuse *me*," Nancy said.

"Miss Drew! I'm so sorry!"

Nancy looked up to see Christopher Hurley, an expression of concern on his tanned face.

"I was in a hurry," he said, holding out his hand to help her up. "But I should have been more careful." He easily hoisted Nancy to her feet.

Against her wishes, Nancy felt her anger subside. "What are you doing here?" she asked.

"Checking on Donna, as usual," Chris said with a smile. He turned to George. "It's George Fayne, right?"

George nodded. "I was in the car when you sent that chess piece hurtling after us."

Chris pointed to himself in mock surprise. "Who, me? I'm sure Donna's told you some wild things about me, but I'm just a coach, trying to put together a winning team for my school in a couple of years."

Spectators began leaving the room. It seemed that most of the afternoon matches were over.

Chris and the two girls stepped away from the door to let people pass.

"You seem pretty interested in getting Donna to quit chess," Nancy said.

Chris stuck his hands in his pockets. "I'm not trying to get her to quit. I want her to focus on track in college and for a few years after that. That's all."

Nancy was skeptical.

"Listen," Chris said. "An athlete is great for only five or six years. Donna could win lots of money as a track star—more than she'll ever make playing chess or being a lawyer or anything else. She could even go to the Olympics someday. After she retires from running she can spend the rest of her life playing chess for all I care."

George crossed her arms. "Shouldn't that be her choice?"

Chris shrugged. "She's young. Sometimes young people need help making decisions."

Nancy tried to surprise Chris. "The outdoor

match last night between Josip and Esther turned out to be more exciting than I expected," she said, watching closely for his reaction.

"Oh, really?" he said. "I'm sorry I missed it." He touched her lightly on the shoulder. "I've got to go." Then he smiled. "See you around, Nancy Drew."

Nancy watched him jog toward the stairs.

"He's got his story down," George said. "Your comment about the match didn't faze him a bit."

Nancy chewed her lower lip. "Hmm. I think he was the other guy in the cloak," she said. "I bet he hired Gary to go crazy during the match."

"What makes you so sure?" George asked.

"For one thing, he knew Gary from working with him unloading chess pieces," Nancy said. "And I would've expected to see him at the exhibition match last night, trying to talk to Donna. I mean, why else did he come all the way down here this week? But he didn't show."

Pushing against the tide of departing spectators, they made their way back into the tournament hall.

All the matches were over. Officials were busy packing up the chessboards and collecting the game clocks.

A man stood at the announcer's table and reminded everyone that the tournament dance was that night at the Ambassador Hotel. Everyone was welcome.

Nancy pointed to the far corner of the room. "Look. There's Bess talking to Eric."

When they got over to Bess, Bess introduced George to Eric.

"I've heard about you," Eric said. "Anna talked about you in her letters home this past year. She admires you very much."

"Thanks," George replied. She lowered her voice. "You must be worried sick about your sister."

Eric's expression changed to a scowl. "Does *she* know, too?" he asked Bess.

Bess nodded.

Eric removed his baseball cap and rubbed his eyes. "Too many people are finding out," he said. "I'm worried the kidnapper is going to do something terrible to Anna."

"Don't panic," Nancy said. "I've got some ideas about who might be involved."

Eric flinched as if he had just received a tiny electric shock. "You do?" he said. "What did you find out? You didn't say anything to the police, did you?"

Nancy was surprised by his reaction. He seemed startled rather than relieved—and more interested in keeping things quiet than finding out where his sister was.

"I don't have anything concrete yet," she said. She decided he was just concerned about the kidnapper's warning not to tell anyone. "And don't worry, Eric—nobody knows about this but us."

"Good," Eric said. "You'll tell me first when you find something out?"

"Of course," Nancy replied. "How's Greta doing? Did she win?"

"Yes," Bess said. She took Eric's hand. "That's got to be a little bit of a relief."

"Yes," Eric agreed. He seemed to relax a little. "She's getting back to her old self." He motioned across the room. "She's over there doing an interview now."

Nancy spotted Brenda Carlton standing between Donna and Greta, holding a miniature tape recorder out as she asked questions.

Nancy excused herself and wandered in that direction.

"How long do you plan to stay in the States?" Nancy heard Brenda ask.

Greta leaned toward the microphone. "Esther Illatavy is my sponsor while I'm here," she said. "I was supposed to stay for the whole summer, but I'm not so sure now."

"Why not?"

Greta shrugged. She seemed much more composed than she'd been the night before. "I miss Holland," she said. "My brother wants to stay and go to college here. He wants to help Esther promote some big chess tournaments here in the States, but I like my home—it's smaller and quieter."

Brenda turned to Donna. "After the first day of competition, you seem like the person to beat."

Donna smiled sheepishly. "It's too early to tell. I'm just playing—"

Nancy was surprised to hear Greta interrupt. "I'm going to crush Donna in the finals," she said.

Donna seemed taken aback by Greta's serious tone of voice. "If you make it to the finals," she shot back.

Brenda had a look of delight on her face. She stepped out of the way, holding only the microphone between the two players.

"Don't worry," Greta said, squaring her slender shoulders. "I'll be up on that center table on Saturday, waiting to take you apart."

"I look forward to it," Donna said. She reached out and clicked off the microphone. "See you then."

Donna marched back to the front of the room so fast Nancy had a hard time catching up to her. She touched Donna on the shoulder.

Donna spun quickly. "Oh, Nancy. It's you."

"Sounded like your interview went well," Nancy said dryly.

Looking back at Brenda and Greta, Donna

broke into a smile. "Esther Illatavy wanted a rivalry. I guess she's got one now."

"You mean that was all an act?" Nancy was incredulous. The anger had seemed so real.

Donna stood close to Nancy. "Greta told me about Anna," she whispered. "And I told her someone's been threatening me."

Nancy grabbed Donna's arm. "Yes. Someone's definitely focusing on the two of you. But now you'll have to be extra careful. Anyone who knows about the kidnapping could be in danger."

Donna nodded gravely. "I know. But if someone's after Greta and me, we're going to put on a good show for them—for now, at least."

"That took a lot of guts," Nancy said.

"We've got you to help us," Donna replied.

The two walked back to where Danitra and Hannah sat chatting.

"Did you ask Greta about where Anna is?" Danitra asked brightly. "I've been looking all over for her."

Donna appeared uncomfortable. It was obvious to Nancy that Danitra had no idea what had happened to Anna.

"Greta said Anna isn't feeling well," Donna said finally. "She's in bed, resting."

"I'll have to give her a call and cheer her up," Danitra said, standing up. She reached over to the seat next to her and picked up the crumpled paper lunch bag the sandwiches had been in. "See a trash can anywhere?"

"Here," Donna said. "I'll take it."

As Danitra handed the bag over, something leaked out, splattering on the floor.

"What a mess," Donna said, opening the sack.

Donna let out a yell and jumped back as if she had seen a snake. The bag dropped to the floor, spraying bright red droplets everywhere.

"What is it?" Nancy asked.

Donna stepped away from the bag, pointing, unable to speak.

Nancy cautiously pulled the bag open. Inside were the four rooks from Donna's chess set, soaked in what looked like fresh blood.

# 8

## Dance with Danger

"Who did this?" Nancy gasped, seeing the little hand-carved chariots.

"Goodness." Hannah took a deep breath and turned away for a moment.

Nancy glanced up and spotted Brenda Carlton striding over. Donna's scream had obviously alerted the nosy reporter that something was going on.

Thinking quickly, Nancy grabbed an abandoned tournament schedule from the closest chair and slid it under the soggy lunch sack to keep the bottom from tearing.

Donna already had herself composed, but Nancy thought Hannah still looked upset.

"What's up?" Brenda asked. "Anything my

readers would be interested in?" She almost stepped in the red splatter, but jumped away. "Ugh! What *is* that?"

"It's just ketchup," Nancy said casually, holding the wet bag away from her body. "I like a lot of ketchup on a cheeseburger. I'm afraid I've made a huge mess." She let out a fake laugh.

Brenda grimaced. "That's disgusting, Nancy Drew. How could you eat that?" She turned on her heel and strode off.

Nancy, Hannah, and the Winstons all looked at one another. "Everyone okay?" Nancy finally asked.

The other three nodded.

"Let's get these pieces cleaned off."

In the restroom, Nancy tore the sack apart carefully. "Here's a note," she said, holding up a red-stained slip of paper.

Just like the first one, it was written with cut-out magazine letters:

Don't defy me! Lose, or it will be a bloody mess!

Danitra almost gagged. "Is that real blood?"

"No," Nancy said. "But it's not ketchup, either. She dipped her finger into some of the goo and held it to her nose. "Smells like plastic," she said. "I think it's fake blood, like they use in movies. It wouldn't be too hard for someone to find."

She handed the four clean rooks to Donna. "This was a pretty grisly warning."

That evening, after a subdued dinner, the two older girls decided that they would rather go to the dance than mope around at home.

The gathering was to take place in the Ambassador ballroom, which meant Nancy would have the opportunity to act on a plan she and George had worked out that afternoon. Since almost everyone associated with the tournament would be down in the ballroom dancing, the rooms upstairs would be empty—the perfect time to do some investigating.

After calling Bess and George, Nancy changed into a skirt, white turtleneck, and a rust-colored jacket.

"I love that jacket!" Danitra said when Nancy came downstairs. "It brings out the red in your hair."

"Thanks. Are you sure you don't want to come with us?"

Danitra shook her head. "If Anna's not going to be there, I'd rather stay home with Hannah and watch a movie or something."

"I'm glad you're staying here," Hannah said from her place on the couch. "I'd be too frightened to be by myself."

Just then Donna came downstairs. She was wearing a pale yellow dress with matching flats. "Ready?"

"Absolutely," Nancy replied. "The question is," she added as they headed for the door, "is everyone ready for us?"

The Ambassador was a big, grand hotel. It was located on a prominent corner directly across the street from the convention center.

Bess and George met Nancy and Donna under the brightly lit awning at the front entrance. A doorman in a green jacket with yellow epaulettes held the door open for them.

"This is the perfect place for the dance," George said as they walked across rich red carpet toward the grand ballroom.

"Yes," Donna said. "Pretty much all the competitors are staying here—on the fifth and sixth floors, I think."

As they entered the ballroom, each girl was handed a card about five inches by seven inches.

"What's this?" Bess asked.

Nancy looked at her card. It was a picture of a chess piece—a white bishop.

"I'm the king," George said grandly.

Donna laughed and held up her card. "I'm a knight."

"I guess we'll find out soon why we have these," Nancy said. "What'd you get, Bess?" she asked, then gestured toward the circular tables with elegant white tablecloths that were placed around the perimeter of the room, leaving the center clear for dancing.

Bess held her card to her chest as they found a table and sat down. "I'm not saying," she replied.

"Oh, come on, Bess," George teased, reaching for the card.

"All right, all right. I'm a lowly pawn," Bess said, holding out the picture.

About forty tournament participants hovered around in groups, talking and drinking punch. A disk jockey in a black tuxedo worked on setting up his sound system.

After a few minutes Esther Illatavy took the microphone from the deejay's stand and addressed the growing crowd.

"Welcome," she said. "We've decided to try something a little different tonight. It may seem silly at first, but I hope it will end up being fun."

She went on to explain why everyone had been given the chess picture cards when they came in. "Everyone has to dance the first dance with someone whose card matches his or hers," she said, smiling. "After that you can stand against the wall or dance with anyone you want."

Nancy saw Bess roll her eyes. "Great," she said. "I get to go looking for a nice, cute pawn."

The lights dimmed and the deejay put on a slow song.

"Okay," Esther called. "Everybody up out of your chairs. Let's dance!"

The first person to get up was Bess. "Well, here goes nothing," she said.

Nancy got up and showed her card around. "Any bishops?"

Two young men started toward her at the same time. One elbowed his way past the other. "This is my dance," he said, handing Nancy his card. The other young man turned away, clearly dejected.

"Maybe next song," Nancy called out.

Her match turned out to be a sixteen-year-old player named William. He was friendly but talked very quickly, and Nancy had to concentrate to understand what he was saying.

Nancy scanned the room. Bess had found a plump boy of about nine or ten years old. Bess was clearly disappointed, but when she saw Nancy, she smiled and waved.

It looked as though Donna was having better luck. She'd found a tall, handsome guy who looked like a model or a competitive swimmer.

When the song ended, Nancy thanked William politely and went looking for George.

She found her friend getting a drink of punch.

"Time to sneak out," Nancy said quietly.

George nodded and put down her glass. As the next song came on, they slipped out of the ballroom and headed for the elevator.

Nancy pushed the button for the fifth floor. "I heard Esther say she was in Room Five-sixteen."

When the elevator doors opened, Nancy stuck her head out cautiously. The hallway was clear.

She stepped out. A gold-colored sign on the wall indicated that number 516 was to the left. The two girls headed in that direction.

Esther's room turned out to be directly across from the ice machine.

"Keep a lookout," Nancy said, pulling a credit card from her pocket.

George took a few steps down the hall. "Be careful, Nan."

The lock was one of the new ones that had a slot for a coded key card. Nancy ran her fingernail down the crack between the door and the frame. Just enough room.

She slid the credit card into the crack and worked it down, trying to trip the bolt.

George stood at the corner, looking down the next hallway. "Hurry," she said.

"Almost got it." Nancy pushed on the card, forcing it in farther.

It snapped in half.

"Hurry!" George said as she rushed to Nancy's side. "Someone's coming."

Nancy heard a door open and close in the next hall.

"I've got to get the rest of my card out," she whispered. "It's stuck."

The girls heard footsteps.

Nancy freed the broken card and shoved it in her pocket just as Norris Stricker came around the corner, carrying an ice bucket.

"Hey! Hi there, Coach Stricker," Nancy said.

The man looked up, startled. "Oh, hello, Miss Drew, Miss Fayne. What are you two doing up here?"

"Looking for Greta van Leeuwen's room," George said quickly. "We heard Anna was sick and we wanted to drop off this card." George held up her chess picture card, careful to show only the blank side to Stricker.

"I don't know which room is hers," Stricker said, sticking his bucket under the funnel of the ice machine. He paused for a second. "But I thought I saw Anna down in the lobby earlier today. She didn't look sick to me."

This startled Nancy. "Are you sure?"

Stricker scratched his scalp thoughtfully. "No, maybe not. She and Greta look a lot alike. Perhaps it was Greta I saw."

"Thanks," Nancy said. "We'll keep looking."

"Good night," Stricker said as he went back to getting his ice.

Nancy and George hurried to the elevator.

"That was a close one," Nancy said. "Good thinking."

Back at the dance, Nancy saw that Bess had somehow managed to land a dance with Eric van

Leeuwen. They acted as if they were having a good time. Nancy was happy to see that Bess was helping keep Eric's mind off his missing sister.

Nancy went to get some punch. As she reached for the ladle, someone snatched it away.

It was Chris Hurley, dressed in a coat and tie. He took Nancy's cup and filled it for her.

"Having fun?" he asked.

"How did you get in here?" Nancy asked.

"This dance is open to anyone with a pass to the whole tournament," Chris said. He pulled a card from his jacket pocket and flipped it over in front of Nancy's face. It showed a white bishop.

"I believe this means you owe me a dance, Miss Drew."

"That was only for the first dance," Nancy answered. "But okay," she said. "I'll dance with you *if* you'll answer some questions."

Chris led her gracefully out onto the dance floor. "Ask whatever you like."

"What do you know about the chess set Donna's grandfather gave her?"

Chris made a quick turn as they danced past another couple. Nancy felt herself nearly being lifted off her feet.

"I know she takes it wherever she goes," Chris said. "She loves it."

Nancy looked into Chris's pale blue eyes. "Did you steal it?"

He stopped midstep, squeezing Nancy's hand

tightly. "No! Did someone take it? Who could do something that nasty and mean?"

"I thought it might be you," Nancy said.

"No way," Chris said earnestly. "I know I've done some pretty extreme things to try to get Donna interested in Evanston, but never anything like that."

They started dancing again. Nancy wanted to believe Chris was telling the truth. She wanted to believe everything he said.

After two more songs, Chris led her over to a seat. "I've got to go," he said. "Maybe I'll see you tomorrow?"

"Yes," Nancy said. "I hope so."

She watched him leave the ballroom. Then she decided to follow. He was up to something, and she had to find out what.

Outside, a light rain was falling. Nancy surveyed the dark streets. There was Chris running up the front steps of the convention center.

Nancy jogged across the street. She got to the front door just as it closed behind Chris. She went in.

It was dark inside. Nancy wondered if any events were going on at this time of night.

Listening closely, she heard the sound of footsteps heading up the stairs to the second floor.

He's going to the main exhibition hall, Nancy said to herself. She crept up the stairs. When she got to the top, she caught sight of Chris outside the double doors of the tournament room.

She ducked behind a pillar. He seemed to be using a pocketknife to open the lock. Within seconds he'd disappeared inside.

Nancy waited, and when he finally came out, he was carrying a small box under his arm. The box was the perfect size to hold Donna's chess pieces, Nancy thought.

As Chris started back down the stairs, Nancy stepped out to follow. The heel of one shoe clacked loudly against the hard marble floor.

Chris froze, then took off at a sprint.

Nancy rushed after him.

Instead of turning right and bolting out the front doors, Hurley veered left.

He grabbed at the door to a room, but it was locked. He took off down the hall for the next meeting room.

This time the door opened and he slipped inside.

Nancy moved up to the door slowly. She recognized the sign from the tour she had given Donna. River Heights Custom Motorcycle Show, it read.

Nancy tugged the door open a few inches.

"Who's there?" Chris shouted. "Who's following me? I can explain what I'm doing here."

I'm sure you can, Nancy thought to herself.

Staying as quiet as she could, she darted into the darkened room.

Once the door closed behind her, Nancy couldn't see a thing. She felt around blindly.

Her hands came to rest on something cold. The handlebars to a motorcycle, she quickly realized.

She stepped forward into the darkness.

Her stomach clenched in fear as an angry rumble filled the room. A motorcycle! Someone had started a motorcycle.

Nancy tried to tell from which direction the sound was coming.

The person revved the engine, making the terrifying roar echo off the walls.

Then a headlight came on at the far end of the room. A yellow blade of light cut through the darkness.

The engine raced again, and the light came speeding straight at Nancy.

# 9

## The Missing Pieces

Nancy tried to jump out of the way, but her legs felt as if they were made of lead. She was moving in slow motion.

The motorcycle was only yards away now, and accelerating fast.

At the last second the motorcycle began to skid, its rear wheel fishtailing. The rider was out of control!

Nancy managed to step out of the way as the rider dumped the bike onto its side and slid past, sparks flying up from the floor.

When the bike finally stopped, Nancy was there, hovering over Chris in her karate stance, ready for anything.

Nothing was going to happen, though.

Chris looked up at her helplessly.

"I'm stuck," he said. "Help me lift the bike off my leg."

Nancy relaxed her stance. "You tried to run over me."

"No, I didn't. I mean, I didn't know it was you, Nancy. When I saw you in the headlight I ditched the bike. It was the only way I could miss you."

He tried to pull free but couldn't. "I heard someone following me. I asked who it was, but you didn't answer. Then I found this bike with the key still in it, and I saw my chance to get away. How was I supposed to know you were standing right in front of the door?"

"You've always got an excuse, don't you?" Nancy said. She grabbed the handlebars and pulled with all her strength. The big bike came up an inch or two.

Chris pulled himself clear and stood up. He tested his knee gingerly. "I think I'm okay," he said. "How about you?"

Nancy's heartbeat was almost back to its normal speed. "Fine," she replied curtly. "So what other excuses can you come up with? Why did you break into the exhibition hall just now?"

Chris looked around. "Hold on." He waded out of the small pool of light coming from the bike's headlight. "Here, I found it," he said, his voice sounding strange in the dark. He returned to the light and handed Nancy the box she'd seen him take from the tournament room.

Nancy opened it. Inside were thirty-two chess pieces—an entire set.

"I took one piece each from a big stack of the sets they're using for the tournament," Chris explained. "I was going to give them to Donna. Sort of as a gift, you know, or a souvenir of the competition."

"What about the games tomorrow?" Nancy asked. "The players wouldn't have complete sets."

"Thirty-two players got bounced from the tournament today, remember? They have enough sets to go around." He smiled mischievously. "But the look on the officials' faces when they discover the missing pieces tomorrow morning should be priceless. I wish I could see them."

Nancy closed the box. "You're not going to see it. I'm taking these back right now."

Chris looked disappointed, but he didn't argue.

Nancy helped him get the motorcycle upright, then they went upstairs and left the box on the announcer's table.

"I'll have to come back tomorrow and pay the owner of that bike for the scratches I put on it," Chris said as they walked back to the hotel. He didn't seem concerned about all the explaining he'd have to do.

"You do believe that I would never steal Donna's chess set, don't you?" he asked when they got to the front of the hotel.

"Maybe," Nancy replied. "Maybe not."

Chris smiled. "That's all I can ask for, I guess. Tell Donna I said hello."

Nancy said good night and returned to her friends at the dance.

Friday morning Nancy and Donna got to the convention center extra early. Donna wanted to go over her strategy with Norris Stricker, and Nancy wanted to keep an eye on Stricker—and his new friend, Esther Illatavy.

Donna's coach met them at the entrance to the tournament room. A long line of ticket holders patiently waited behind a velvet rope barrier.

"This is when it gets serious," Stricker said, his eyes sparkling. "There's going to be a standing-room-only crowd today. We're getting down to the best players in the world now."

Nancy pointed to a group of workers who were laying a run of heavy electrical cables out of the room. "What are they up to?"

"Extending the video capabilities to the entire convention center," Stricker replied. "People who can't get seats in the main hall can sit in other rooms around the building and watch the featured matches on TV."

"You'll be able to hear them, too," Donna

added. "They'll be announcing the moves over the intercom system."

"Is it always like this?"

Donna and Coach Stricker both laughed. "No. We always have *some* spectators," Donna said. "But this is one of the biggest tournaments of the year. People will be here from all over the world to see the final match."

Stricker held up his index finger. "That's why it's so important for you to play your best, Donna. You can impress a lot of important people if you win."

Donna looked down at her shoes, then over at Nancy. The pressure finally seemed to be getting to her, Nancy thought.

"Now, chin up!" Stricker scolded. "You must *intimidate* the other players, not evoke their pity." He looked at his clipboard. "You're playing Rachel Weeks this morning, so get yourself prepared."

"You'll do great," Nancy said as Stricker led Donna down the hall to one of a series of smaller rooms that contained practice tables.

Nancy showed her pass and entered the exhibition hall. Finding a chair in a back row where she could see people come and go, Nancy sat down to watch and wait.

She picked out Esther Illatavy right away. The former world champion strode around purposefully, directing the workers who were fixing the video monitors, lecturing the officials for misplacing something, and chatting breezily with contestants and their parents.

At one point there appeared to be some confusion about the morning's matchups. Esther and another official snapped at each other. The official held up a computer printout and pointed to it, but Esther ripped the papers out of his hands and shoved them back in his chest as a wadded-up ball. That seemed to settle the matter.

Nancy waved when she saw Bess, George, and Eric come through the door.

There were only two seats left next to Nancy, and George insisted that Bess and Eric take them. She sat cross-legged on the floor.

Nancy noticed that Eric didn't seem as happy as he had the previous night at the dance. When Nancy had gone back into the ballroom and told her friends about tailing Chris Hurley, Eric had been totally fired up. He was certain that Chris must be the kidnapper and wanted to confront the track coach.

It had taken Nancy a long time to get him calmed down. She'd told Eric that she didn't think Chris was involved.

But now Eric had a sour expression on his face. "So," he said quietly to Nancy, "do you have any good news today? Any strong suspects?"

"Not strong enough," Nancy said, putting him

off as she had before. She didn't want Eric to run over and throw a punch at Esther Illatavy. That wouldn't help them find Anna. "How's Greta doing?" she asked.

"All of a sudden she's totally confident," Bess said.

"Yes," Eric said. "I think she'll win."

At ten o'clock the matches began.

The cameras—and the spectators—focused almost entirely on Donna's match against Rachel Weeks.

Rachel looked older than Donna—perhaps seventeen or eighteen, Nancy thought. She was tall, with straight brown hair, and didn't appear to be easily intimidated. She had no expression at all on her face.

Donna was playing the white pieces, so she had the first move.

Seconds passed, then minutes. Donna still hadn't made her first move. Her game clock ticked steadily down. She stared at Rachel, her hands resting calmly in her lap.

"What's she doing?" Bess asked.

Eric was riveted. "Taking a big chance. If she takes too much time, her clock will run out and she'll lose."

Finally Donna moved one of her pawns forward on the board. The crowd seemed to let out a collective sigh of relief.

Rachel hadn't been fazed one tiny bit. She quickly moved a piece out, then slapped the button on her clock loudly.

Nancy looked at her watch. It was time. The housekeepers would be cleaning the rooms at the Ambassador right about now. She got up, offering George her chair.

"Where are you going?"

"Back to the hotel," Nancy whispered. "Don't let anyone else know, okay?"

George nodded. "Watch out."

As Nancy walked down the hall of the convention center, she heard a soft voice announce Donna's next move over the intercom.

"F2 to F4."

When she got back to the fifth floor of the Ambassador Hotel, Nancy glanced at her watch again. Ten-thirty. She hoped her timing was right.

It was.

As she stepped out of the elevator, she spotted the housekeeper's cart down the hall to her right.

Nancy stole up to the cart, which was piled high with fresh towels and had a big trash bag attached to one end.

The door to the room the housekeeper was making up was open. Nancy could hear the housekeeper inside snapping fresh sheets on the bed.

Nancy searched the top of the cart for the

housekeeper's master key card. She found wash-cloths, water glasses wrapped in plastic, and a stack of ice buckets. No luck—Nancy didn't see the card.

She skirted around the cart and peered into the room. There it was!

The housekeeper's master card—the one that opened all the rooms—lay on the desk next to the phone book.

Nancy flattened herself against the outside of the door frame, waiting for her chance.

When the housekeeper stepped into the bath-room, Nancy knew it was now or never. She darted into the room, grabbed the card, and turned to leave.

The housekeeper stood right in front of her!

No. It was just the woman's reflection in the long mirror on the open bathroom door.

Nancy made her escape. Once in the hall, she had to remind herself to breathe.

She strode quickly to Room 516. The master key worked perfectly, and in seconds Nancy was safely inside Esther Illatavy's room which was already made up.

Nancy went to work, knowing she didn't have much time. The housekeeper would discover the missing card any second.

The desk drawers held only stacks of extra tournament programs and books about chess. More interesting things were in the nightstand.

Nancy found a notebook with lists of cities and dates—mostly during the upcoming summer months.

Names of sponsors were grouped next to each city, each with a number and a dollar sign next to it. Nancy was amazed at the money involved.

One entry read: "Seattle / July 12 / Exhibition Match / Computer Fair / Greta and Donna vs. Computer / $250,000.00."

No wonder Esther and Stricker wanted Greta to stay in the States for the summer.

Nancy put the notebook away and pulled out a computer printout like the one she'd seen Esther and the other official arguing about earlier.

It listed all the participants in the tournament by their point rankings. Donna was at the top with 2,450 points. Greta was next.

But below those two names, things weren't as clear. Esther had crossed out some names and drawn arrows from one to another. Some of the arrows pointed to Greta.

Suddenly Nancy figured out what Esther was doing. She was picking players she thought Greta could beat. Esther was trying to control Greta's matches and set her up to win.

Nancy dumped the printout back in the night-stand and closed it. It had been only a few minutes, but she had to get the card back to the housekeeper.

Nancy slowly opened the door and peeped

out. The housekeeper was still working on the same room.

Nine long strides got Nancy to the cart. She could hear the water running in the bathroom.

Not daring to take the card back into the hotel room, Nancy placed it conspicuously on the stack of face towels. The housekeeper would be surprised to find it there but would probably just tell herself she forgot that she had placed it there.

As Nancy turned to walk to the elevator, she saw something in the big trash bag. She reached in and pulled out a brightly colored chess magazine. She quickly flipped through the pages. Her heart jumped.

Gaping holes glared back at her from where someone had cut out words and letters.

Nancy's heart skipped a beat. Whoever had sent Donna the threatening notes had cut the letters from this very magazine!

# 10

## Hang It Up!

Nancy tucked the magazine under her arm and sprinted for the elevator. As she watched the lights blink off each floor on the way down, Nancy tried to figure out to whom the magazine had belonged.

The housekeeper had already cleaned Esther's room. Stricker's room was around the corner, which meant it had also been made up. The magazine could have come from either of their rooms, or any of the others on that side of the fifth floor.

Rushing back to the convention center, Nancy burst through the double glass doors. She was so preoccupied that she almost ran right into Esther Illatavy.

"Oh, hi," Nancy said, startled. She stepped back. Esther was having a conversation with Eric van Leeuwen, and Nancy realized she'd nearly bowled both of them over.

Nancy tried to fold the magazine over to hide the cover, but it was too late.

Esther raised an eyebrow. "Miss Drew, I see that you're studying chess."

Nancy felt the blood rush to her face, warming her cheeks.

"Yes," she said. "Yes, I'm finding that it's a very interesting game."

"I'm sure," Esther said. "But you can't learn from magazines—you've got to play."

"Which magazine is that?" Eric asked, reaching toward Nancy. "Where did you get it?"

Nancy held it away. "It's just one that Donna gave me," she said.

"Are you sure? Can I see it?" Eric said.

Before Nancy could react, Esther snatched the magazine from her hand.

She held it up for Eric. "See, it's just the latest issue of *American Chess Master*. Do you approve?"

Esther handed the magazine back to Nancy. "He probably has a long list of things he thinks are better for you to read, isn't that right, Eric?"

"No. Well, maybe," Eric said.

"Well, tell her all about it later," Esther said.

"Right now, you and I have to talk about your sister and how she's playing."

Nancy nodded goodbye, taking the chance to excuse herself. She bolted upstairs.

Had Esther recognized the magazine? She was so icy cool it was impossible to tell. Eric had certainly been interested, but that probably didn't mean anything.

At the exhibition hall Nancy had to weave her way through a throng of standing spectators five or six people deep.

She found Bess and George. Greta was sitting in the seat Eric had occupied earlier.

"Greta!" Nancy said. "Did you win?"

Greta smiled. "In sixteen moves."

"She was awesome," Bess whispered, holding up her fist. "It took only twenty minutes."

"Donna's still playing," George said, anticipating Nancy's question.

Nancy turned her attention to the center table, then to the nearest video monitor.

The view was from directly over the table. Nancy could see the chessboard, the clock off to the right side of the screen, and Donna's and Rachel's hands at the top and the bottom.

Nancy searched the vast room for Norris Stricker but didn't see him anywhere. That didn't mean anything, she decided. The room was too crowded to know if any one person was there.

The video monitor showed Rachel's hand

reach across the board. She picked up her knight, jumped it over Donna's bishop, and placed it on a square close to one of Donna's rooks.

F5 to G3 flashed on the monitor.

Nancy knew that the knight was the only piece that could jump over other pieces, but the move still surprised her. She always had a hard time seeing where the knight would land on its required L-shaped move—up two squares in one direction, one in another.

"Donna's got to get her rook out of there," Greta whispered. "Rachel's knight can take it on the next move."

Donna's clock was ticking. She didn't move a muscle. The only sound was the players on the long tables moving their pieces and hitting their clocks: *click, chok . . . click, chok . . . click, chok.*

Then Donna's hand flashed over the table. Instead of moving her rook, she took her bishop and ran it diagonally almost all the way across the board, taking one of Rachel's pawns.

"Check!" she said firmly.

When spectators realized where the bishop had ended up, a murmur of approval rose up. Someone on the far side of the room clapped loudly three or four times, then stopped.

Bess looked at Greta. "What happened?"

Greta had a look of amazement on her face. "A perfect fork. I didn't see it at all."

Greta explained the situation. "That bishop

moves diagonally," she said. "Look what pieces Rachel had on two of the diagonals leading away from Donna's bishop."

Nancy studied the board. Donna's bishop looked as if it were a person standing at a fork in the road, trying to figure out which road to take. If it traveled along the black diagonal squares to the left, it would run into Rachel's king. If it chose the right fork, there was Rachel's queen.

"Rachel has to move her king," Nancy said. "She has to get him out of check."

Greta nodded. "And that means she loses her queen—the most powerful piece on the board."

That's what happened.

Rachel moved her king off the black diagonal, and Donna took the queen with her bishop.

With her fingertip, Rachel gently toppled her own king. She stood up abruptly and held her hand out to shake Donna's.

A few spectators burst into applause, while others tried to hush them up—there were other matches going on, after all.

"Why did she knock over her own king?" Bess asked.

"She conceded the game," Greta said. "She knew there was no way she could beat Donna once she lost her queen."

Donna waved in appreciation of the applause, then made a few distinct motions with her hands.

Nancy knew Donna was sending a message to

Danitra in sign language. She looked in the direction Donna had signed.

There were Danitra and Hannah, sitting a few rows over.

Nancy checked her watch. It was nearly twelve o'clock. "You guys want to get some lunch?"

"Count me in," George said.

Bess nodded and turned to Greta. The petite Dutch girl smiled shyly. "Thanks, but I think I'll wait for Eric."

"Okay," Bess said. "We'll be here to silently cheer you on again at your afternoon match."

Greta ran a hand through her hair. "Great. I need a cheering section."

Nancy led the way to the front of the room, waving to catch Donna's attention as she walked.

"You hungry after that amazing victory?" Nancy asked as they met up at the door.

"Famished," Donna replied. Again, she had an armload of bouquets from fans.

"How about Danitra?"

"She wants to stay till the end of the matches," Donna said.

Nancy, Donna, Bess, and George all trooped out into the bright midday sun.

As they got close to Nancy's car, Nancy scoped the area to make sure no one was around.

"Take a look at what I found at the Ambassador," she said, unfolding the magazine.

The other three girls gathered around as

Nancy opened the pages and displayed the missing letters.

"The notes!" Donna gasped. "Whose was this?"

"That's what I don't know," Nancy said. "The housekeeper dumped it out of someone's wastebasket, but I don't know whose."

They got to the Mustang and Nancy pulled out her keys. "It could be Esther Illatavy's or . . ." She hesitated to tell Donna her suspicions about Norris Stricker. "Or it could have come from about ten other rooms on that floor of the hotel."

Nancy put her key in the lock of her door and turned it. Nothing happened. "Strange," she said. "I must have forgotten to lock my door this morning."

"Esther Illatavy?" Donna was saying as she walked around to the passenger side of the car. "I can't believe that. What does she have against me?"

George and Bess climbed into the backseat. "I don't think it's anything against you," Nancy said. "But she seems very interested in helping Greta win the tournament."

All conversation stopped as Nancy settled into the driver's seat.

Three chess pieces—a white pawn, a white bishop, and a black king—hung from the rearview mirror, dangling by tiny nooses. A note taped to the dashboard read:

Donna:

Tell your three snooping friends to hang it up!

"No way!" George said in disbelief. She put one hand on Bess's shoulder and the other on Nancy's. "Those are the three chess pieces we dressed as for the dance last night."

Nancy picked up the note. This one was printed, just like the one the kidnapper had sent to Greta.

Nancy looked at Donna. "It looks like the same person is after both you and Greta."

"And now us," Bess said fearfully.

After calling the police and answering questions for twenty minutes, the girls didn't have much appetite. Nancy practically had to force Donna to have a bowl of soup so she'd have enough energy for her afternoon match.

"If someone wants me to lose before I get to the final they're going to have to do a little better than this," Donna said. She dropped her spoon into her soup in disgust.

"You're so brave about this," Bess said, taking a sip of iced tea. "I'd be swearing off chess forever if this were happening to me."

"It's so cowardly," Donna said. "I wish this idiot would face me in person."

Soon it was time for Donna to prepare for her next match.

"I feel sorry for Donna's next opponent," Nancy confided to George as they returned to the convention center.

Sure enough, Donna tore through her match like a chess demon. She sent her major pieces—bishops, knights, and rooks—fearlessly out onto the center of the board. She was an army general without reserve or remorse.

The young man facing her didn't have a chance. Checkmate came before he knew what had hit him.

Greta won her afternoon match as well, setting the stage for Saturday, the final day of the tournament.

At home that night, while Danitra was downstairs watching TV, Nancy explained her suspicions about Esther Illatavy to Donna.

"I heard her talking to Coach Stricker," Nancy said, sitting on the edge of her bed. "They seem to be planning some kind of huge tour for this summer."

"Yeah, right," Donna said. She was playing with a chain of paper clips at Nancy's desk. "Coach Stricker comes up with a new plan every week. The only problem is that he never bothers to ask me what I want to do."

"I saw some notes in Esther's hotel room. She's got dates booked already. There's all kinds of money involved. If Greta goes back to Holland, that all disappears. No tour, no rivalry between you two that gets more girls interested in chess."

"If Greta wins and gets a lot of money and attention, she might want to stay here," Donna said. "I get it." She added another paper clip. "So Esther wants to make sure Greta wins by kidnapping Anna and scaring me half to death."

"I think so," Nancy said.

"That's one way to start a rivalry," Donna mused.

"There's also Chris Hurley," Nancy said. "I haven't ruled him out, either."

"This is all so crazy." Donna tossed the paper clips aside and stood up. "I'm going for a run to clear my head. You want to come?"

"That's a great idea. I'll get my shoes."

The two friends stretched out on the front porch, Nancy in blue running shorts and a white, lightweight nylon jacket, Donna in a red outfit.

It was late when they started out, but the full moon gave off a warm glow, and they felt safe running together. After a half mile or so, Donna pulled a white headband from her pocket and put it on to keep her hair out of her eyes.

"You're a pretty good runner, Nancy," she said as they picked up the pace.

Nancy grinned. "I do a little running now and then. Let's head for the river. It's beautiful at night."

Donna agreed, and they sped up even more, their long, graceful strides covering long sections of pavement. They ran through a quiet residential neighborhood, passing in and out of the green pools of light cast by streetlamps.

Nancy took a look back over her shoulder and saw a green sedan about two blocks back. She led the way up onto the sidewalk.

As they ran, Nancy kept expecting to hear the green car approach and then pass them by as it moved down the street.

She glanced back again. The car was still holding back, matching their pace perfectly—only now the headlights were off.

Nancy scanned the road ahead. Totally deserted.

"Donna," she said, "don't slow down. I think someone's following us."

# 11

## Pawns in a Dangerous Game

Donna checked behind her. "What should we do?" she whispered.

"Keep running," Nancy said. They were close to downtown River Heights now, and Nancy kept an eye out for other people.

She glanced back again. "Whew! The car's gone now, Donna. Must've been a false alarm."

Donna laughed. "We're getting paranoid."

They passed downtown shops—a bakery, a bank, a department store. The windows were all dark, except for the low glow of security lights.

A young couple crossed the street ahead of them, and a solitary runner came toward them from a few blocks away but turned down a side street, moving fast.

Nancy began to feel more relaxed. "This jog was a good idea," she said. "I feel better already."

Donna agreed. "I like to try to think about nothing while I run," she said. "It helps me unwind."

They took a right at the convention center and headed toward Riverside Park.

"We'll circle the park and come back along the river," Nancy said.

Before Donna could answer, bright headlights snapped on less than a hundred yards in front of them.

The girls heard an engine fire to life. Tires squealed, and the car raced toward them, gaining speed.

"It's the car that was following us!" Nancy yelled.

The driver swerved up onto the sidewalk.

Nancy and Donna leaped clear as the car whooshed past, missing them by inches.

The driver hit the brakes and spun the sedan around.

Donna grabbed Nancy's sleeve. "He's coming back to try again!"

The girls jumped over a park bench and headed for the safety of the park's tall trees.

"He can't get the car in here," Nancy said.

A few seconds later they found themselves on the painted grass of the outdoor chessboard. The life-size chessmen stood as they had at the end of Josip and Esther's game.

The teens crouched down behind a knight and looked back toward the street.

"The car's parked," Donna said. "It's just sitting there."

"Yes, but it's empty," Nancy whispered. "Where's the driver?"

Donna shook her head. "I don't see him anywhere."

The yellow moonlight made the ancient chess pieces look like glossy figures in a wax museum. The heavy brows hooded the eyes of the bishops and kings, making the chessmen appear expressionless, remote.

"I don't like this at all," Nancy said. She left the row of white pieces and walked out into the middle of the chessboard. "I don't see anyone," she whispered, continuing over to the black queen. She turned and saw Donna, still next to the knight. Rising up behind her was the shape of a man in a cloak.

"Donna!" Nancy yelled. "Behind you!"

Donna screamed. She sprinted toward Nancy. The two girls hid behind the queen, searching the chessboard frantically.

"Now I don't see him," Nancy whispered. "Where is he?"

Donna pointed diagonally across the board. "There! There, I saw him!"

Nancy thought she spotted a dark figure pass silently between two chess pieces.

"We might be able to make a run for it," she said. "Or, we could play his game—try to surprise him."

"Retreat or attack," Donna murmured. Then the look in her eyes hardened. "Coach Stricker is always telling me to be more aggressive. I say attack."

"Good," Nancy said. "I'll decoy."

Donna stayed hidden while Nancy walked out boldly to a rook in the middle of the board. She stood there, watching.

Nancy didn't have to wait long. A few seconds later the cloaked figure stepped out of the shadows, the long hood hiding his face.

"What do you want?" Nancy asked. She got no answer.

The figure stepped forward, letting his hands come free of the folds in the long robe. The cold steel of a dagger glinted in the moonlight.

Nancy wanted to keep the hefty rook between herself and the attacker. They circled the seven-foot chess piece twice. Each time the thug tried to get around in one direction, Nancy would nimbly dart away.

When the cloaked figure stopped for a second, it was all the time Donna needed. Nancy saw her friend bolt out from the darkness.

Donna ran up to the thug and kicked him behind his knee. His leg collapsed, and he went down with a groan of pain.

With a karate yell, Nancy pushed the rook as hard as she could. The heavy chess piece tilted, stalled, then tipped over.

The robed figure rolled clear as the rook crashed into the turf. He scrambled to his feet, knife ready.

"Hey! What's going on here?"

Nancy looked up. A jogger had come running over from the street.

That moment of hesitation was all the culprit needed. He sprinted off toward the river.

Nancy and Donna gave chase. They reached the flood wall and stopped. Clouds had covered the moon, and it was almost totally dark now.

"Do you see him?" Nancy asked, catching her breath. She listened for footsteps but heard only the lapping of the water against the wall.

"No," Donna replied. "There's no way to tell which direction he went. Well," she said with a sigh, "I guess I got my wish. Whoever's after me isn't using notes anymore—now it's a knife."

The jogger who had interrupted the fight caught up to them. "Donna! Nancy! You okay?"

It was Chris Hurley.

"Yes, we're fine," Nancy said.

As the three of them walked back across the park to the street, Nancy explained what had happened.

"Good thing I showed up when I did," Chris said. "He didn't seem to like the odds of three against one, even with that blade."

"Hey," Donna retorted. "Nancy and I had things under control."

"Knowing you, I'm sure you did," Chris said seriously. "But I'm still glad I got here before you had to prove it. What was that all about, anyway? Why is some freak in a black cloak after you guys?"

"Somebody wants Donna out of the tournament," Nancy replied.

Chris started looking for a public phone so he could call the police. "Why don't you drop out then, Donna?" he asked. "There'll be plenty of other tournaments."

"Believe me," Donna said. "I'm starting to consider it."

"Where'd you come from, anyway?" Nancy asked. "Was that you running down Court Street a little while ago?"

"Yup. I was just sitting around in my hotel room and thought I'd go for a run around the park. Sounds like you two had the same idea."

At the intersection next to the convention center, Nancy spotted a passing police cruiser and waved for it to stop.

After they reported the incident, Chris said good night and jogged off toward his hotel. Nancy and Donna got a ride home with the officer.

The officer asked the girls to call immediately if they saw anyone suspicious hanging around or if Donna received another note.

"Don't worry," Donna said. "We will."

They thanked the officer and headed up the front steps to Nancy's house.

"Well, looks like Coach Hurley's innocent," Donna remarked.

"Yes," Nancy agreed. She had to admit she was relieved. Yet there was still someone out there— someone holding Anna van Leeuwen and planning a new way to harm Donna Winston.

The tournament semifinals were Saturday morning. Only four players remained: Donna, a fourteen-year-old girl from Tucson, a seventeen-year-old boy from New York, and Greta, who'd played her way back up from the losers' bracket.

Donna was up at six in the morning. Nancy found her down at the kitchen table, using an old chess set of Carson Drew's to go over her strategy and memorize various chess moves her opponent might use to open the match.

"Nervous?" Nancy asked, pouring herself some orange juice.

"A little," Donna admitted. "Not so much about the match. More about what might happen to Anna. I think I might withdraw."

"You still don't know that Greta's going to win," Nancy said. "Maybe you should try to get to the finals this afternoon. Then, if Greta makes it, too, you can decide."

Donna sat quietly, thinking. "Okay," she said

finally. "That's what I'll do. I'll play my best this morning."

Nancy was glad to see Donna's confidence return.

Two hours later Nancy, Donna, and Danitra were ready to drive over to the convention center.

As Nancy opened the door leading from the kitchen out to the garage, there was a loud knock at the front door.

Nancy heard Hannah answer. She was about to continue to the car, when Hannah's singsong voice floated through the kitchen: "Donna, don't leave yet. It's something for you."

The girls returned to the living room. Nancy felt her heart racing. She hoped it wasn't another package from the person terrorizing Donna.

"It's a beautiful bouquet of roses," Hannah said. "Must be from a fan who wants to wish you well before the match today."

Nancy relaxed. What a relief.

Donna took the bouquet from Hannah, grinning.

"Maybe it's from Mom and Dad," Danitra said.

As Donna reached for the attached note, her smile vanished.

A single white pawn from her missing chess set dropped to the floor.

Donna shifted the rose stems.

Another pawn dropped . . . and another.

All sixteen pawns fell to the carpet one by one, like tiny people abandoning a sinking ship.

# 12

## A Player Surrenders

Donna removed the note and read it aloud, her voice shaking with anger.

"This is your final warning. Lose today or face the consequences. Sacrifice a pawn early in the morning match so I know you understand."

"What does that mean, sacrifice a pawn?" Hannah asked.

Donna tossed the bouquet on the couch and sank into one of the deep cushions, her head in her hands. "A sacrifice is when you give up one of your pieces when you don't need to," she said.

"You sacrifice to try to trick your opponent into doing something he might not normally do."

Danitra helped her sister by picking up the pawns and placing them on the coffee table.

Nancy studied the note. It bore the logo of a local florist. Going to the phone, she called them up.

"River Heights Floral," a voice said.

"Hi," Nancy said. She gave them her address. "Did someone order roses delivered to my house?"

She heard the sound of shuffling papers.

The voice came back on. "Yes. Didn't you get them?"

"I got them," Nancy replied. "I was wondering if you could tell me the name of the person who placed the order."

"I wish I could," the man said. "That was an unusual order. If he ordered by phone I'd have his name and credit card number, but I found a package at the front door this morning."

"A package?"

"Yes. A box with some chess pawns in it. There was cash and a note telling us to put the pawns into a bouquet and send them to you. Is there some kind of problem?"

"No. Everything's fine." Nancy thanked the man and hung up.

Next she called the police. They offered to send a car over, but she refused.

"I don't think you need to," she said. "But it might be good to have a couple of extra officers at the chess tournament today."

"I'll see to it," the dispatcher said.

Nancy returned to the living room. "Donna," she said. "What do you want to do?"

Donna stood up. "I want to play some chess. Let's go."

At the semifinals that morning, all four players sat at the center table. The long tables the contestants had been using until that point had been removed to make room for more spectators. A video camera hung suspended over each of the two remaining chessboards.

With special reserved tickets they'd gotten from Donna and Greta, Nancy and Danitra joined George, Bess, and Eric in seats close to the front.

Donna sat staring at her opponent, eighteen-year-old Max Currie. Greta looked as if she hadn't slept all night. Then again, Nancy thought, her rival, Marie Planck, a girl from Arizona, didn't look much more rested. She nervously twirled her finger at her temple, twisting and untwisting a single lock of hair.

"I think Greta will play well today," Eric said. He held his baseball cap in his hands.

"We studied tapes of her opponent last night," he said. "Marie always plays the same style."

Bess put her hand on Eric's shoulder. "Everything's going to turn out all right," she said softly.

He looked at the floor and took a deep breath. "I hope so."

The matches started. Greta and Max, who were playing the white pieces, hit their clocks.

Donna seemed to start more tentatively than usual, while Greta raced to an early lead, taking two of Marie's pawns and a knight.

Nancy watched Donna's match closely. Would she sacrifice a pawn, as the note had told her to?

Both Donna and Max played slowly, their hands hovering over the chessmen on every move.

Max moved one of his bishops out three diagonal squares, and suddenly Nancy saw Donna's chance.

If she moved one of her pawns forward, Max would be able to take it. Whoever was terrorizing Donna would know she planned to lose.

Apparently Donna saw it, too. She put her hand over the pawn, then paused.

Nancy felt herself biting the inside of her cheek.

Donna moved her knight instead.

That's it, Nancy thought. She's playing to win.

She did win. Within an hour only two of the original players remained: Donna Winston and Greta van Leeuwen.

\* \* \*

124

The final match was to begin at five in the afternoon. Carson Drew and Howard Winston had called right after lunch to say that they were driving down from Chicago and hoped to be at the convention center for the start of the game. Mr. Winston had asked Nancy and Danitra to leave them two reserved seat tickets at the booth on the first floor.

"It's hardly worth it," Donna said mournfully. "There isn't going to be any match worth watching."

Donna had decided to lose to Greta on purpose, hoping that the kidnapper would release Anna unharmed. The plan was to wait until the start of the match was announced. Donna would make a few moves, then concede.

"At least I'll get second place," she said.

By the time Nancy and Danitra got to the convention center that afternoon, the crowd was so big that people had spilled out into conference and meeting rooms all over the building. These spectators would watch the matches on the remote video monitors that had been hooked up.

As Nancy and her friends were getting comfortable in their front row seats, she noticed Chris Hurley leaning against a far wall. She waved. He smiled and nodded toward her.

The center table was now set up on a three-foot-high platform so the crowd could see more easily.

Donna and Greta sat in uncomfortable-looking straight-back chairs at the back of the platform, waiting for Esther to introduce them and ask them to take their places at the chessboard.

Norris Stricker and Esther stood next to the platform discussing something. They shook hands, then Esther climbed the stairs to the microphone.

"I'm so worried about Anna," Bess said under her breath. "And can you imagine how her exchange family feels? She's been living with the Codys for almost a year, and now she disappears. They must be worrying like crazy. And what are they telling Anna's parents? Anything at all?"

Nancy felt as if someone had just hit her over the head with a sledgehammer. "Bess! You're right!"

"About what?" Bess looked confused.

"I've got to check something out," Nancy whispered. "I'll tell you later."

Turning to Danitra, Nancy grasped her hand firmly. "Get your sister's attention," she said. "Send her a message in sign language."

"What?" Danitra asked.

"Tell her not to lose the match right away. Tell her to keep it going for as long as she can. I'll be back soon."

Danitra nodded.

As Esther introduced Donna and Greta, two

little girls dressed as queens climbed the platform steps to deliver flowers to each player.

Nancy fought through the crowd, sprinting all the way to her car. She drove back to her own neighborhood. It just doesn't make sense, she said to herself as she wheeled onto her street. Why hadn't the Codys called the police? Had the kidnapper sent them a threatening note as well? She needed to talk to them. They might have the clue she needed to put everything together.

Nancy swung into the Codys' driveway and slammed on the brakes.

She jumped out and ran to the front door. "Come on . . . come on. Be home," she pleaded after she'd rung the bell.

A pleasant-looking woman with short brown hair answered the door.

"Well, hello, Nancy," Mrs. Cody said, drying her hands on a dish towel. "How are you?"

Nancy didn't have time for polite greetings. "Mrs. Cody, do you know where Anna is?"

"Of course, Nancy. She's at the Ambassador Hotel." Worry crossed Mrs. Cody's face. "Why? Is something wrong?"

"No, no," Nancy replied. "But I need to know. When did she go there?"

"Three days ago. When her brother and sister got into town," Mrs. Cody said. "She wanted to stay with Greta and Eric while they were here,

127

and we said it was okay, of course. I just talked to her on the phone an hour ago."

"Do you happen to know what room she's staying in?"

"Room Five-oh-four. Are you sure there's nothing wrong?"

"Don't worry, Mrs. Cody," Nancy said as she ran back to her car. "I'll call and explain later."

Nancy rocketed back to the Ambassador Hotel. If Anna was there it would mean that she'd never really been kidnapped. She and Eric must have staged the whole thing. But why? To force Greta to win the tournament? And if that was what had happened, then who was after Donna? The attack at the park had definitely been real.

When she arrived at the hotel, Nancy ran to the elevator. As it went up it seemed to be stuck in super slow motion. Nancy stood right at the door, waiting impatiently for it to open.

When the bell rang at the fifth floor, Nancy bolted out the doors. Room 504 was down the same hall as Norris Stricker's room. Stopping in front of it, Nancy paused. She had to be right. Anna had to be in there. Stepping carefully away from the peephole, Nancy rapped on the door hard.

Nothing. She pounded it with her fist.

"Who's out there?" a small voice asked.

It was Anna.

"Anna!" Nancy said. "It's Nancy Drew! Open the door, now!"

"No. I can't. I mean, no, my name's not Anna. You must have the wrong room."

"I don't have the wrong room," Nancy shouted. "Now open the door before I call the police and have them break it down."

Anna opened the door.

Nancy stepped in and slammed the door behind her. Grabbing Anna by the arm, Nancy sat the younger girl down on the bed.

"What's going on, Anna?"

Anna put her hands over her face and started to cry. "I knew the plan wouldn't work," she sobbed.

"What wouldn't work?" Nancy asked.

"Eric's plan," Anna said, tears running down her face. "Greta told us she wanted to lose the tournament. She said she wanted to go home."

Nancy handed the girl a tissue.

"Eric wanted her to win so we could all tour the country with her. He said he and Greta could make a lot of money and I'd get to stay here after my exchange year is over."

"So you faked your own kidnapping," Nancy said.

"Yes. We wanted to make Greta win."

"And what about Donna Winston?"

Anna nodded. "Eric stole her chess set. He

didn't think Greta could beat her, even playing her best. So he wanted to scare her into dropping out."

"Well, it didn't work." Nancy turned to go. "You know, that was a pretty cruel thing to do to your own sister," she said.

"I know," Anna said. "But that's not the worst part."

Nancy paused.

"Eric's out of control," Anna continued. She stood up and went over to the nightstand. Picking up the notepad next to the phone, she tore off the top sheet and handed it to Nancy. "A copy of this note is in the flowers that were given to Donna at the beginning of the game."

Nancy read the note.

I've played games long enough. Now I have now I have Danitra. If you ever want to see her alive again, lose the match!

# 13

## Queen's Gambit

Nancy crumpled the note. "What's his plan?"

Anna began to cry again. "He's wearing a costume. He's disguised as a king," she said.

Nancy remembered the person she'd seen hanging around outside the exhibition room entrance.

"I don't know where he's taking Danitra," Anna continued. "He wouldn't tell me. I don't think even he knows what he's going to do."

"Who else is involved?"

Anna sank back down on the bed. "No one. Just me and Eric."

"Okay," Nancy said. "You stay right here." She went to the door. "If you want to do the right thing, Anna, call the police now and tell them to meet me at the convention center."

Anna sniffled and went to the phone.

On the elevator ride back down to the lobby, Nancy went over the events of the past three days. If only Eric and Anna were involved, it meant Eric had been the person who attacked her and Donna in the park. It meant the magazine with the letters missing had come from Anna's room.

Nancy remembered what Norris Stricker had said when he was getting ice. He said he thought he'd seen Anna in the lobby of the hotel, but he couldn't be sure. Nancy almost laughed. It must have been hard for Anna to stay cooped up in the hotel room for almost three whole days.

She'd probably gotten bored and gone exploring around the hotel. After all, what would it matter if someone saw her. Only Greta was supposed to know about the kidnapping. Anna's exchange family knew she was hanging out in the hotel. The only person they needed to fool was Greta.

That first night when Greta told Bess and Nancy—that was when Eric's wild plan had started to unravel. With other people wondering where Anna was, Eric had had to escalate his original simple plan into something dangerous and complicated.

Nancy ran across the street to the convention center.

Police Chief McGinnis met her at the entrance to the exhibition hall.

"What's going on?" he asked, keeping his

voice low. "We got a call about a kidnapping. Someone told us to meet you here."

"Yes," Nancy said. "Follow me."

Chief McGinnis looked annoyed, but he stayed close to Nancy as she worked her way through the crowd to the front row.

The first thing she noticed when she got there was that Danitra's seat was empty. Nancy looked up at the platform and caught Donna's eye. Nancy could tell she was terrified—she'd obviously received the note. Reading the look on Donna's face, Nancy nodded and mouthed the words "Yes. Keep playing as long as you can. We'll find Danitra."

When Donna seemed to understand, Nancy kneeled down next to Bess's chair. "Where's Danitra?" she whispered.

"She got paged," Bess said, not knowing anything was wrong. "Right after you left, the announcer paged her and told her there was a message for her at the ticket booth. She said it must be her father and took off."

Nancy and Chief McGinnis rushed from the room.

Out in the hall, McGinnis got on his radio. "Station, this is the chief. We've got a kidnapping. A missing girl by the name of . . ."

"Danitra Winston," Nancy said. "The guy who took her is named Eric van Leeuwen."

"Station, send units to the airport, the bus

133

station, and the train station," McGinnis said. "Don't let anyone leave." With Nancy's prompting he gave a description of Danitra and Eric.

A video monitor on a rolling TV stand sat outside the exhibition room. A group of people watched the match intently.

Watching the match on the monitor made Nancy suddenly realize something.

"Forget about the bus station," she said. "They aren't there. They're here!"

"Hold on," Chief McGinnis said into his radio. He released the Talk button. "What are you saying?"

Nancy moved away from the monitor. She didn't want to alarm the spectators.

"The kidnapper is watching the game on TV," Nancy explained. "He has to know what's happening, who's winning. That means he's still somewhere in the convention center."

Chief McGinnis seemed skeptical, but he got back on his radio. "Send two more units here," he said. Then he switched channels. "All units, start a search of the convention center—top to bottom."

As Chief McGinnis began organizing his officers, Nancy went over to the video monitor. "How's the match going?"

"The Dutch girl's doing well," a tall, grayhaired man said. "Look at this." He pointed to Greta's two knights and one of her bishops. "She's got control of the center of the board." He traced a diagonal line away from the bishop and a couple of L shapes going away from the knights. "I don't see how Donna can get past this wall here. Pretty soon she'll be trapped."

"Donna's wasting too much time," another man said. "She's taking five or ten minutes between each move. It's as though she's waiting for the right move to fall out of the sky to her."

Nancy didn't let on to how right the man was. She had to hurry. If the match ended before they found Danitra, two things could happen: Eric might release Danitra unharmed, or—well, she didn't like thinking about any other possibilities.

Bess had said Danitra had been paged to go down to the ticket office. Nancy ran down the stairs to see if the person working the ticket booth had seen anything unusual.

"No." The man shook his head. "I've been here all afternoon. I can't say I've seen anything out of the ordinary."

Nancy thanked him. Where should she look? There had to be a hundred different rooms in the convention center.

As she walked back toward the stairs, Nancy spotted something sticking out of the trash can by the door of the men's restroom. A green hat. Eric's baseball cap, she said to herself as she pulled it out. He must have changed into the king disguise in the bathroom.

She stood holding the cap in her hands as Eric had that morning.

Where were they?

Nancy smiled to herself, then broke into a run, taking the stairs three at a time. When she got to the second floor, she jogged on past the exhibition hall.

"Hey! What's going on?" Chief McGinnis called.

"No time to talk," Nancy replied.

Nancy rounded the corner with Chief McGinnis in tow. She stopped under the sign at the next big event space—the dog show.

Inside, a man in a black suit was unleashing a yellow Labrador retriever. The dog sat quietly. Then the man stepped away from the dog. He made a small hand signal and the dog jumped up and went to his master's side.

The crowd clapped loudly.

Nancy strode into the room, turning to the nearest spectator. "Where are the other dogs?"

"Huh?"

"The dogs waiting to compete or perform or whatever it is they do next," Nancy said in exasperation. "Where are they?"

The man appeared to be baffled. "The next room over."

Nancy strode out and continued down the hall.

"What in the world are you doing?" McGinnis asked.

Nancy didn't answer.

The next room was a large, carpeted lounge practically big enough to play softball in.

About forty people were running their dogs through their paces, practicing before being called out in front of the judges.

Nancy saw the dog she wanted. A short woman with curly auburn hair stood near the center of the room. A floppy-eared beagle sat at her feet, looking up at her expectantly.

Nancy jogged over to the woman. "I'd like to borrow your dog," she said.

The woman looked aghast. "I should think not, young lady."

Nancy took the leash. "I'm sorry. I don't have time to argue. Here," she said, grabbing a couple of doggie yummies out of the woman's hand. "I might need a few of those, too."

She turned to leave, but the woman seized the leash. "Give me back my Biscuit!"

Chief McGinnis interrupted, holding up his badge. "Police business, ma'am. Let the dog go."

As McGinnis argued with the woman, Nancy and Biscuit walked away.

Once they were out in the hall, Nancy gave the beagle a treat and scratched behind his brown ears. "Okay, Biscuit," she said. "It's time to do some really important work."

She pulled Eric's baseball cap from her pocket

and held it under the dog's nose. "Find him, Biscuit," Nancy ordered. "Find Eric."

Biscuit immediately ran forward on his stumpy little legs. He headed directly toward the chess tournament, then made a turn and stood looking down the stairs.

Nancy followed him down to the first floor.

There Biscuit trotted over to an elevator about twenty yards from the ticket booth.

"Good boy," Nancy said, pushing the button.

They got on the elevator. "Now which way? Up or down?"

Biscuit just looked up at her, panting.

"Down," Nancy said. She pushed the button for the basement.

The door opened to a long hallway. Water pipes and heating ducts ran along the ceiling, and the only sound was the whine of the massive air conditioner. Just ahead, a sign on the wall read Danger: High Voltage.

Nancy held the leash tight. Biscuit whined and tugged. He'd picked up the scent again. Nancy looked in the direction the dog was pulling her.

Steel doors were evenly spaced down the length of the hallway. They must be behind one of those doors, Nancy thought.

She let the beagle tow her along. He stopped at the fourth door down and pawed at the cement floor.

"Shh!" Nancy said, giving the dog the last treat.

She put her ear to the door. It was heavy steel, but Nancy thought she heard the sound of voices.

She had no other choice. Taking a deep breath, she put her shoulder against the door and shoved it open.

"Nancy!" Danitra yelled.

Nancy took in the scene with one glance. The room was a small maintenance area. Danitra sat in a chair at the back wall.

Still in his king disguise, Eric stood next to a small wooden workbench.

At the sight of Nancy, he grabbed his knife off the table. In one long stride, he was next to Danitra, threatening her with the knife.

"Don't come any closer!" he shouted.

Nancy pretended not to know who he was. She figured as long as he thought his identity was a secret, he'd have no reason to harm her or Danitra.

"Let her go," Nancy said, keeping her voice steady.

"King's rook. H6 to F6," a voice said.

Eric jumped as if startled.

Nancy spotted where the voice had come from. A video monitor sat on the workbench next to a chess set.

Eric edged back over to the table. He moved a black rook two spaces to the left.

"I see you're tracking the game," Nancy said. "Who's winning?"

"Greta van Leeuwen."

Eric was obviously nervous. He kept glancing back and forth between Nancy and Danitra.

Nancy felt the dog brush against her ankle as it ran into the room.

Eric jumped again in surprise.

Nancy took her chance. Rushing forward, she kicked Eric's wrist. The knife clattered to the floor.

Eric dived for it, but a cold voice boomed out from the doorway: "Police! Don't move a muscle!"

It was Chief McGinnis.

Nancy bent down and ripped the mask off. "I knew it was you, Eric," she said. "It was a tough match, but you lost."

She and Danitra let McGinnis finish up with Eric and Biscuit. They had one more piece of business to take care of.

The two girls hurried back upstairs to the exhibition hall. As they passed the TV monitor outside the door, Nancy heard the announcer say, "C4 to E3. Check!"

Nancy stopped. "Who?" she asked.

The tall gray-haired man turned to look at her. "Greta just put Donna in check. Looks like the match is just about over."

# 14

## Checkmate

"We have got to get to where she can see us!" Danitra cried. "I need to show her I'm okay."

The girls made their way to Bess and George in the front row.

When Donna spotted Danitra, first her eyes went wide, then she broke into a huge smile.

Danitra pointed to herself, then formed two sign language letters, *O* and *K*, telling her sister that she was fine.

"Tell her that Anna's okay, too," Nancy said.

Bess jumped up with such excitement that the man in the seat behind her told her to sit down. She did, but the happiness still showed on her face.

Danitra was confused. "Of course Anna's okay. She's just feeling bad, that's all."

Nancy realized that they'd never told Danitra about the kidnapping. "I'll explain later," she said. "Just tell Donna. She'll understand—and it will make her play better, I promise."

Danitra relayed the message.

Donna reacted by leaning over and whispering something to Greta.

Greta almost seemed to faint with happiness. She looked gratefully over at Nancy.

By now the officials and some of the spectators were wondering what was going on. A man in a red vest came over to Nancy's row and whispered harshly that the girls should keep quiet and not disturb the players.

But Danitra said one more thing in sign language, finishing by knocking her fists together twice in front of her body.

Donna responded with another smile, then a firm nod.

"What did you say?" Nancy asked.

"I told her to win the game," Danitra said.

George looked up. "The first thing she has to do is get out of check," she said doubtfully.

By now Donna was far behind. One rook, one knight, and three pawns were spectators on her side of the board. Greta had lost only a pawn and a knight.

Donna studied the board. She moved her king one square over, rescuing him from immediate danger.

Nancy studied the players' positions on the board. From what she could tell, the tall man outside had been right—Donna was going to have a tough time breaking through Greta's defenses.

Greta advanced a pawn one space forward, patiently closing in on Donna's king.

Donna moved her one remaining rook back to its original starting position.

"What is she doing?" Nancy wondered.

In a quiet whisper Danitra said, "It looks like she's retreating. Coach is really upset."

Danitra was right. Stricker sat in a chair behind the match officials' table. Nancy watched him cringe. He seemed to want to jump out of his chair, run up to the chessboard, and make Donna's moves for her.

The expression on Greta's face changed. It went from a tight, thin-lipped, concentration to a slight smile. She pushed her glasses up into place and reached for her bishop.

She slid the piece all the way down to Donna's end of the board. She kept her hand on the bishop's head while she assessed the new position.

Nancy held her breath. As soon as Greta took

her hand off the bishop, she wouldn't be able to take the move back. And, Nancy thought, that move might be a mistake.

Nancy tried to picture what the next few moves would be. Yes, Donna's retreat might have been a brilliant way to trick Greta into letting her pieces advance unprotected.

Greta let go of the bishop.

Donna quietly moved her king forward one space.

A few people in the crowd murmured.

"Quiet, please," an official said.

By moving her king up one space, Donna had opened a direct lane from her rook to two of Greta's pieces: the bishop, and right behind it, a knight. It was a perfect skewer, just as Donna had explained when they'd found the knives stuck in her chessboard.

Greta's smile disappeared. She had no choice. If she moved her bishop, Donna's rook would take her knight; if she didn't move the bishop, Donna would take it.

She moved the bishop.

Donna took the knight and slapped the button on her clock loudly.

"Now things are a little more even," Danitra said.

But Donna still had a long way to go. She and Greta fought evenly for a while, Donna moving especially quickly to make up for lost time on her clock.

Donna's speed seemed to distract Greta. She began playing nervously with her hair. At one point, she took her glasses off and rubbed the bridge of her nose.

Donna kept bringing her pieces back to her side of the board. Nancy figured she must just be wishing to protect her king.

Another half hour into the match, both players were down to only a few pieces. They each had four pawns, a bishop, a rook, and a queen.

"It's dead even," George whispered.

Nancy nodded. Donna had her major pieces— her bishop, her rook, and her queen—all close to her king at her side of the board.

Greta seemed to have the advantage—her pieces were aggressively attacking Donna. Only her bishop was back on her side of the board. Greta moved her queen even farther into Donna's territory.

Nancy felt a burning sensation in the pit of her stomach. It looked as if Donna was done for.

Donna was going to lose her rook and be in check on Greta's next move. She had to move her king, Nancy thought. Get him out of danger.

Donna didn't move her king. She moved her queen, sending it all the way across the board to the same row as Greta's king.

"Check!" Donna said.

Greta didn't seem fazed, and as far as Nancy could tell, this was only a stay of execution. Greta would move her bishop back one space, putting it between her king and Donna's queen. Then she could proceed with her attack.

Sure enough, Greta moved her bishop.

Donna took Greta's queen.

The crowd erupted.

"Quiet, please!"

"What a fantastic move!" Danitra cried. "Donna forced her to move the bishop."

Bess looked confused. "What happened? I missed it."

"When Greta moved her bishop to get her king out of check, it left her queen unprotected," Nancy explained. "Donna was only pretending she was after Greta's king. The target the whole time was the queen."

Once Greta lost her queen, the match was soon over. Donna won in three more moves.

The spectators jumped to their feet, cheering. They gave both players a long standing ovation.

Late that night Nancy, Bess, George, and the Winston girls lounged around the Drews' living room, much too excited to go to bed.

It turned out that Carson Drew and Howard Winston had made it to the convention center in time to see the end of the match. Mr. Winston had been very proud of Donna—and grateful to Nancy. But now the two men had gone to Mr. Drew's study to let the girls talk.

A two-foot-high gold trophy in the shape of a king's crown sat on the coffee table. *Donna Winston—International Junior Master Chess Champion* had already been engraved on the base.

"I really thought Norris Stricker and Esther Illatavy were involved," Nancy was saying. She sat next to Donna and George on the couch. Danitra relaxed in an overstuffed chair.

"Yes," George said. "What about that conversation you overheard through the bathroom vent?"

"And the notebooks in her hotel room?" Danitra asked.

Nancy took a sip of her soft drink. "She and Stricker were hoping to make a bunch of money with a big promotional tour for Greta and Donna, but there's nothing unlawful in that."

"But what about her saying she could guarantee Greta would get to the finals?" George asked.

"It turns out she was using her power as tournament director to pick opponents for Greta whom she thought Greta could beat."

"Isn't that against the rules?"

Donna nodded. "The International Chess Federation is going to have some tough questions for her, but what she did isn't nearly as bad as kidnapping."

Danitra laughed. "Not quite!"

The phone rang, and Hannah's voice floated in from the kitchen. "Donna! It's for you."

As Donna got up, Nancy looked at Bess, who sat quietly sulking on the floor. "Are you sad about Eric?"

Bess nodded. "I still can't believe he would do those horrible things."

"It just got out of control," Nancy said. "I don't think he meant for it to get so bad."

A few minutes later Donna returned. "That was Greta," she said, sitting down. "She found the rest of my chess set in Eric's hotel room. I can pick it up tomorrow."

"What's happening with Anna and Eric?" Nancy asked.

"She thinks the authorities are going to send Anna home to Holland. Greta's going, too."

"That's what Greta always wanted," George said.

Donna nodded. "She says Anna's sad about it, but considering what she helped put us all through, it's pretty light punishment."

"What about Eric?" Bess asked.

"He's in more trouble," Donna said. "Greta thinks he never meant to really hurt anyone, but the police are still sorting out his story. He may be prosecuted here."

The doorbell interrupted their conversation.

Nancy glanced at her watch. "Who could that be at this hour?" She got up and answered the door. It was Chris Hurley.

"Hi," Nancy said, and invited him in.

"I'm heading back to Chicago," he said, stepping into the living room. "I just wanted to make sure Danitra was okay—and say goodbye to you, Nancy."

"I'm fine," Danitra said with her usual mischievous smile. "But Donna's decided to quit chess. She told me she's going to Evanston College after high school to run track."

Chris's eyes went wide. "Really?"

"No way!" Donna said, laughing. "I've had enough of chess *and* running."

"Yes," Nancy said. "You should try something totally new, Donna. How about ballet?"

**Do your younger brothers and sisters
want to read books like yours?**

**Let them know there
are books just for *them!***

They can join Nancy Drew and her best
friends as they collect clues and solve
mysteries in

## THE
# NANCY DREW
## NOTEBOOKS ®

Starting with

**#1 The Slumber Party Secret**

**#2 The Lost Locket**

**#3 The Secret Santa**

**#4 Bad Day for Ballet**

**AND**

**Meet up with suspense and mystery**

**in Frank and Joe Hardy:**

**The Clues Brothers™**

Starting with

#1 The Gross Ghost Mystery

#2 The Karate Clue

#3 First Day, Worst Day

#4 Jump Shot Detectives

Look for a brand-new story every
other month at your local bookseller

A MINSTREL® BOOK

Published by Pocket Books                1366-02

# THE HARDY BOYS® SERIES  By Franklin W. Dixon

| | | |
|---|---|---|
| ☐ #69: THE FOUR-HEADED DRAGON | 65797-6/$3.50 | |
| ☐ #71: TRACK OF THE ZOMBIE | 62623-X/$3.50 | |
| ☐ #72: THE VOODOO PLOT | 64287-1/$3.99 | |
| ☐ #75: TRAPPED AT SEA | 64290-1/$3.50 | |
| ☐ #86: THE MYSTERY OF THE SILVER STAR | 64374-6/$3.50 | |
| ☐ #87: PROGRAM FOR DESTRUCTION | 64895-0/$3.99 | |
| ☐ #88: TRICKY BUSINESS | 64973-6/$3.99 | |
| ☐ #90: DANGER ON THE DIAMOND | 63425-9/$3.99 | |
| ☐ #91: SHIELD OF FEAR | 66308-9/$3.99 | |
| ☐ #92: THE SHADOW KILLERS | 66309-7/$3.99 | |
| ☐ #93: SERPENT'S TOOTH MYSTERY | 66310-0/$3.99 | |
| ☐ #95: DANGER ON THE AIR | 66305-4/$3.50 | |
| ☐ #97: CAST OF CRIMINALS | 66307-0/$3.50 | |
| ☐ #98: SPARK OF SUSPICION | 66304-6/$3.99 | |
| ☐ #101: MONEY HUNT | 69451-0/$3.99 | |
| ☐ #102: TERMINAL SHOCK | 69288-7/$3.99 | |
| ☐ #103: THE MILLION-DOLLAR NIGHTMARE | 69272-0/$3.99 | |
| ☐ #104: TRICKS OF THE TRADE | 69273-9/$3.99 | |
| ☐ #105: THE SMOKE SCREEN MYSTERY | 69274-7/$3.99 | |
| ☐ #106: ATTACK OF THE VIDEO VILLIANS | 69275-5/$3.99 | |
| ☐ #107: PANIC ON GULL ISLAND | 69276-3/$3.99 | |
| ☐ #110: THE SECRET OF SIGMA SEVEN | 72717-6/$3.99 | |
| ☐ #112: THE DEMOLITION MISSION | 73058-4/$3.99 | |
| ☐ #113: RADICAL MOVES | 73060-6/$3.99 | |
| ☐ #114: THE CASE OF THE COUNTERFEIT CRIMINALS | 73061-4/$3.99 | |
| ☐ #115: SABOTAGE AT SPORTS CITY | 73062-2/$3.99 | |
| ☐ #116: ROCK 'N' ROLL RENEGADES | 73063-0/$3.99 | |
| ☐ #117: THE BASEBALL CARD CONSPIRACY | 73064-9/$3.99 | |
| ☐ #118: DANGER IN THE FOURTH DIMENSION | 79308-X/$3.99 | |
| ☐ #119: TROUBLE AT COYOTE CANYON | 79309-8/$3.99 | |
| ☐ #120: CASE OF THE COSMIC KIDNAPPING | 79310-1/$3.99 | |
| ☐ #121: MYSTERY IN THE OLD MINE | 79311-X/$3.99 | |
| ☐ #122: CARNIVAL OF CRIME | 79312-8/$3.99 | |
| ☐ #123: ROBOT'S REVENGE | 79313-6/$3.99 | |
| ☐ #124: MYSTERY WITH A DANGEROUS BEAT | 79314-4/$3.99 | |
| ☐ #125: MYSTERY ON MAKATUNK ISLAND | 79315-2/$3.99 | |
| ☐ #126: RACING TO DISASTER | 87210-9/$3.99 | |
| ☐ #127: REEL THRILLS | 87211-7/$3.99 | |
| ☐ #128: DAY OF THE DINOSAUR | 87212-5/$3.99 | |
| ☐ #129: THE TREASURE AT DOLPHIN BAY | 87213-3/$3.99 | |
| ☐ #130: SIDETRACKED TO DANGER | 87214-1/$3.99 | |
| ☐ #132: MAXIMUM CHALLENGE | 87216-8/$3.99 | |
| ☐ #133: CRIME IN THE KENNEL | 87217-6/$3.99 | |
| ☐ #134: CROSS-COUNTRY CRIME | 50517-3/$3.99 | |
| ☐ #135: THE HYPERSONIC SECRET | 50518-1/$3.99 | |
| ☐ #136: THE COLD CASH CAPER | 50520-3/$3.99 | |
| ☐ #137: HIGH-SPEED SHOWDOWN | 50521-1/$3.99 | |
| ☐ #138: THE ALASKAN ADVENTURE | 50524-6/$3.99 | |
| ☐ #139: THE SEARCH FOR THE SNOW LEOPARD | 50525-4/$3.99 | |
| ☐ #140: SLAM DUNK SABOTAGE | 50526-2/$3.99 | |
| ☐ #141: THE DESERT THIEVES | 50527-0/$3.99 | |
| ☐ #142: LOST IN GATOR SWAMP | 00054-3/$3.99 | |
| ☐ #143: THE GIANT RAT OF SUMATRA | 00055-1/$3.99 | |
| ☐ #144: THE SECRET OF SKELETON REEF | 00056-X/$3.99 | |
| ☐ #145: TERROR AT HIGH TIDE | 00057-8/$3.99 | |
| ☐ THE HARDY BOYS GHOST STORIES | 69133-3/$3.99 | |
| ☐ #146: THE MARK OF THE BLUE TATTOO | 00058-6/$3.99 | |
| ☐ #147: TRIAL AND TERROR | 00059-4/$3.99 | |
| ☐ #148: THE ICE-COLD CASE | 00122-1/$3.99 | |
| ☐ #149: THE CHASE FOR THE MYSTERY TWISTER | 00123-X/$3.99 | |
| ☐ #150: THE CRISSCROSS CRIME | 00743-2/$3.99 | |
| ☐ #151: THE ROCKY ROAD TO REVENGE | 02172-9/$3.99 | |
| ☐ #152: DANGER IN THE EXTREME | 02173-7/$3.99 | |
| ☐ #153: EYE ON CRIME | 02174-5/$3.99 | |

## LOOK FOR AN EXCITING NEW
## HARDY BOYS MYSTERY COMING FROM
## MINSTREL® BOOKS

Simon & Schuster, Mail Order Dept. HB5, 200 Old Tappan Rd., Old Tappan, N.J. 07675

Please send me copies of the books checked. Please add appropriate local sales tax.
☐ Enclosed full amount per copy with this coupon (Send check or money order only)
☐ If order is $10.00 or more, you may charge to one of the following accounts: ☐ Mastercard ☐ Visa
Please be sure to include proper postage and handling: 0.95 for first copy; 0.50 for each additional copy ordered.

Name _____

Address _____

City _____ State/Zip _____

Books listed are also available at your bookstore. Prices are subject to change without notice.      657-31

# NANCY DREW® MYSTERY STORIES By Carolyn Keene

| | | |
|---|---|---|
| ☐ #58: THE FLYING SAUCER MYSTERY | 72320-0/$3.99 | |
| ☐ #62: THE KACHINA DOLL MYSTERY | 67220-7/$3.99 | |
| ☐ #68: THE ELUSIVE HEIRESS | 62478-4/$3.99 | |
| ☐ #72: THE HAUNTED CAROUSEL | 66227-9/$3.99 | |
| ☐ #73: ENEMY MATCH | 64283-9/$3.50 | |
| ☐ #77: THE BLUEBEARD ROOM | 66857-9/$3.50 | |
| ☐ #79: THE DOUBLE HORROR OF FENLEY PLACE | 64387-8/$3.99 | |
| ☐ #81: MARDI GRAS MYSTERY | 64961-2/$3.99 | |
| ☐ #83: THE CASE OF THE VANISHING VEIL | 63413-5/$3.99 | |
| ☐ #84: THE JOKER'S REVENGE | 63414-3/$3.99 | |
| ☐ #85: THE SECRET OF SHADY GLEN | 63416-X/$3.99 | |
| ☐ #87: THE CASE OF THE RISING STAR | 66312-7/$3.99 | |
| ☐ #89: THE CASE OF THE DISAPPEARING DEEJAY | 66314-3/$3.99 | |
| ☐ #91: THE GIRL WHO COULDN'T REMEMBER | 66316-X/$3.99 | |
| ☐ #92: THE GHOST OF CRAVEN COVE | 66317-8/$3.99 | |
| ☐ #93: THE CASE OF THE SAFECRACKER'S SECRET | 66318-6/$3.99 | |
| ☐ #94: THE PICTURE-PERFECT MYSTERY | 66319-4/$3.99 | |
| ☐ #96: THE CASE OF THE PHOTO FINISH | 69281-X/$3.99 | |
| ☐ #97: THE MYSTERY AT MAGNOLIA MANSION | 69282-8/$3.99 | |
| ☐ #98: THE HAUNTING OF HORSE ISAND | 69284-4/$3.99 | |
| ☐ #99: THE SECRET AT SEVEN ROCKS | 69285-2/$3.99 | |
| ☐ #101: THE MYSTERY OF THE MISSING MILLIONAIRES | 69287-9/$3.99 | |
| ☐ #102: THE SECRET IN THE DARK | 69279-8/$3.99 | |
| ☐ #104: THE MYSTERY OF THE JADE TIGER | 73050-9/$3.99 | |
| ☐ #107: THE LEGEND OF MINER'S CREEK | 73053-3/$3.99 | |
| ☐ #109: THE MYSTERY OF THE MASKED RIDER | 73055-X/$3.99 | |
| ☐ #110: THE NUTCRACKER BALLET MYSTERY | 73056-8/$3.99 | |
| ☐ #111: THE SECRET AT SOLAIRE | 79297-0/$3.99 | |
| ☐ #112: CRIME IN THE QUEEN'S COURT | 79298-9/3.99 | |
| ☐ #113: THE SECRET LOST AT SEA | 79299-7/$3.99 | |
| ☐ #114: THE SEARCH FOR THE SILVER PERSIAN | 79300-4/$3.99 | |
| ☐ #115: THE SUSPECT IN THE SMOKE | 79301-2/$3.99 | |

| | |
|---|---|
| ☐ #116: THE CASE OF THE TWIN TEDDY BEARS | 79302-0/$3.99 |
| ☐ #117: MYSTERY ON THE MENU | 79303-9/$3.99 |
| ☐ #118: TROUBLE AT LAKE TAHOE | 79304-7/$3.99 |
| ☐ #119: THE MYSTERY OF THE MISSING MASCOT | 87202-8/$3.99 |
| ☐ #120: THE CASE OF THE FLOATING CRIME | 87203-6/$3.99 |
| ☐ #121: THE FORTUNE-TELLER'S SECRET | 87204-4/$3.99 |
| ☐ #122: THE MESSAGE IN THE HAUNTED MANSION | 87205-2/$3.99 |
| ☐ #123: THE CLUE ON THE SILVER SCREEN | 87206-0/$3.99 |
| ☐ #124: THE SECRET OF THE SCARLET HAND | 87207-9/$3.99 |
| ☐ #125: THE TEEN MODEL MYSTERY | 87208-7/$3.99 |
| ☐ #126: THE RIDDLE IN THE RARE BOOK | 87209-5/$3.99 |
| ☐ #127: THE CASE OF THE DANGEROUS SOLUTION | 50500-9/$3.99 |
| ☐ #128: THE TREASURE IN THE ROYAL TOWER | 50502-5/$3.99 |
| ☐ #129: THE BABYSITTER BURGLARIES | 50507-6/$3.99 |
| ☐ #130: THE SIGN OF THE FALCON | 50508-4/$3.99 |
| ☐ #131: THE HIDDEN INHERITANCE | 50509-2/$3.99 |
| ☐ #132: THE FOX HUNT MYSTERY | 50510-6/$3.99 |
| ☐ #133: THE MYSTERY AT THE CRYSTAL PALACE | 50515-7/$3.99 |
| ☐ #134: THE SECRET OF THE FORGOTTEN CAVE | 50516-5/$3.99 |
| ☐ #135: THE RIDDLE OF THE RUBY GAZELLE | 00048-9/$3.99 |
| ☐ #136: THE WEDDING DAY MYSTERY | 00050-0/$3.99 |
| ☐ #137: IN SEARCH OF THE BLACK ROSE | 00051-9/$3.99 |
| ☐ #138: THE LEGEND OF THE LOST GOLD | 00049-7/$3.99 |
| ☐ NANCY DREW GHOST STORIES | 69132-5/$3.99 |
| ☐ #139: THE SECRET OF CANDLELIGHT INN | 00052-7/$3.99 |
| ☐ #140: THE DOOR-TO-DOOR DECEPTION | 00053-5/$3.99 |
| ☐ #141: THE WILD CAT CRIME | 00120-5/$3.99 |
| ☐ #142: THE CASE OF CAPTIAL INTRIGUE | 00751-3/$3.99 |
| ☐ #143: MYSTERY ON MAUI | 00753-X/$3.99 |
| ☐ #144: THE E-MAIL MYSTERY | 00121-3/$3.99 |
| ☐ #145: THE MISSING HORSE MSYTERY | 00754-8/$3.99 |
| ☐ #146: GHOST OF THE LANTERN LADY | 02663-1/$3.99 |

## A MINSTREL® BOOK

## Published by Pocket Books

**Simon & Schuster, Mail Order Dept. HB5, 200 Old Tappan Rd., Old Tappan, N.J. 07675**
Please send me copies of the books checked. Please add appropriate local sales tax.
☐ Enclosed full amount per copy with this coupon (Send check or money order only)
☐ If order is $10.00 or more, you may charge to one of the following accounts: ☐ Mastercard ☐ Visa
Please be sure to include proper postage and handling: 0.95 for first copy; 0.50 for each additional copy ordered.

Name _____

Address _____

City _____ State/Zip _____

Credit Card # _____ Exp.Date _____

Signature _____

Books listed are also available at your bookstore.  Prices are subject to change without notice.        760-30